Alfred Gatty

The circle of blessing

and other parables from nature

Alfred Gatty

The circle of blessing
and other parables from nature

ISBN/EAN: 9783743373785

Manufactured in Europe, USA, Canada, Australia, Japa

Cover: Foto ©Andreas Hilbeck / pixelio.de

Manufactured and distributed by brebook publishing software (www.brebook.com)

Alfred Gatty

The circle of blessing

AUTHORITY AND OBEDIENCE.

Circle of Blessing.

THE CIRCLE OF BLESSIN[G]

AND OTHER

PARABLES FROM NATURE.

BY

MRS. ALFRED GATTY,

AUTHOR OF " WORLDS NOT REALIZED," " PROVERBS ILLUSTRATED,"
" AUNT JUDY'S TALES," ÆTC.

NEW YORK:

GENERAL PROTESTANT EPISCOPAL SUNDAY SCHOOL
UNION AND CHURCH BOOK SOCIETY,
762 BROADWAY.

1861.

CONTENTS.

PREFACE.

"THERE are two books," says Sir Thomas Browne, in his *Religio Medici*, "from whence I collect my divinity: besides that written one of God, another of his servant, Nature — that universal and public manuscript that lies expanded unto the eyes of all: those that never saw Him in the one have discovered Him in the other." And afterwards, as if giving a particular direction to the above general statement, he adds: "Those strange and mystical transmigrations that I have observed in silkworms turned my philosophy into divinity. There is in these works of Nature, which seem to puzzle reason, something divine, and hath more in

1*

it than the eye of a common spectator doth discover."

Surely these two passages, from the works of the celebrated physician and philosopher, may justify an effort to gather moral lessons from some of the wonderful facts in God's creation: the more especially as St. Paul himself led the way to such a mode of instruction, in arguing the possibility of the resurrection of the body from the resurrection of vegetable life out of decayed seed: "Thou fool, that which thou sowest is not quickened except it die!" *Thou fool*—fool! not to be able, in thy disputatious wisdom, to read that book of "God's servant, Nature," out of which there are indeed far more actual lessons of analogy to be learned than we are apt to suppose or can at once detect. Assuredly, the changes of the silkworm, and the renewal of life from the vegetable seed, are not more remarkable than the soaring butterfly arising from the earth grub,—a change which, were the caterpillar a reasonable being, capable of contemplating its own existence, it would reject as an impossible fiction.

It was not, however, Sir Thomas Browne's remarks which gave rise to these Parables; for the first was written in an outburst of excessive admiration of Hans Andersen's *Fairy Tales*, coupled with a regret that, although he had, in several cases, shown his power of drawing admirable morals from his exquisite peeps into nature, he had so often left his charming stories without an object or moral at all. Surely, was the thought, there either is, or may be devised, a moral in many more of the incidents of nature than Hans Andersen has traced ; and on this view the "Lesson of Faith" was written—an old story ; for the ancients, with deep meaning, made the butterfly an emblem of immortality—yet to familiarize the young with so beautiful an idea seemed no unworthy aim.

"The Sedge Warbler" is open to the naturalist's objection, that female birds do not sing. But it suited the moralist that they should do so in this particular case; and one may be content to err in such company as Spenser, Milton, Thomson, Beattie, and the immortal Izaak Walton.

> " And in the violet-embroidered vale,
> Where the love-lorn nightingale
> Nightly to thee *her* sad song mourneth well."
> *Song of Comus.*--MILTON.

> " And Philomele *her* song with teares doth steepe."
> *The Shepherd's Calendar, Nor.*—SPENSER.

> " But the nightingale, another of my airy creatures, breathes such sweet, loud music out of *her* instrumental throat, that it might make mankind to think that miracles had not ceased."—WALTON's *Angler.*

> —— " All abandon'd to despair, *she* sings
> Her sorrows through the night; and on the bough
> Sole sitting, still at every dying fall
> Takes up again *her* lamentable strain."
> THOMSON'S *Seasons—Spring.*

> "And shrill lark carols clear from *her* aërial tour."
> BEATTIE'S *Minstrel.*

An interesting account of the first discovery of the Sedge Warbler, of its habit of singing by night as well as by day, of its mocking notes, and of its distinctive differences from the Reed Warbler, may be found in White's *History of Selborne.*

Nothing but the present growing taste for the use of the microscope, and the study of zoöphytes, among other minute wonders of sea, earth and sky, could justify the selection of so little popular a subject for a parable as will be found in " Knowledge not the limit of Belief."

" The moon that shone in Paradise," was the exclamation of a very melancholy mind, which failed to recognise in the thought the hope it was calculated to convey, and which it has now been attempted to teach.

May the " Lesson of Faith" and the " Lesson of Hope" each work its appointed end ; and may they combine to enforce on the mind of youth the value of " that still more excellent gift of charity," which " hopeth all things, believeth all things, endureth all things !"

The Circle of Blessing.

INTRODUCTION.

A PASSENGER-SHIP was passing through the region of equatorial calms. For days she had lain under an atmosphere of oppressive vapour. The sea wore a leaden, inky hue, and at two or three miles' distance from the vessel, air and ocean seemed to melt into each other. A sort of hot steaminess prevailed, which soaked through clothes, sails, and every article on board, and produced the most wretched languor and depression in every one subject to its influence.

People bore it according to their age, experience, and habits of self-control. The old sailors, who knew what they had, at times, to expect in those latitudes,—either from burning heat, suffocating mists, or drenching rains, contented themselves with wringing out their clothes, and enduring patiently what could not be avoided or altered. Several of the passengers, new to the trial, made the nearly vain experiment of plunging into sea-water for refreshment ; but even sea-water seemed to have lost its magically tonic power here, where it was most needed, under the burning ardours of the Line.

Others, irritated by their sensations, irritated themselves yet more by vehement expressions of annoyance and disgust. They railed against their ill-luck, in having left home so as to encounter such detestable weather in their voyage ; abused themselves as fools for having subjected themselves to such a risk, and looked up with faces clouded over with wrath and reproof at those " *intolerable and accursed mists*," which hung, truth to say, above and around the vessel on every side, with a thickness through which no eye could pierce.

A young man had but just uttered that ill-conditioned phrase, when a passenger, of somewhat advanced age, and a demeanour calmed to serenity by knowledge and reflection, came up to him, and, although he was a stranger, spoke. "Young man," said he, "cease to dishonour God by such almost blasphemous complaints. Look up, rather, at those mists, and bless Him that they are there. You are indebted to them for the very bread which has supported your life up to this hour of your ignorant ingratitude."

And the man, advanced in years and wisdom, passed forward along the deck, and left the youth speechless among his astonished companions.

No explanation was given, and not another word of outward murmuring was heard. The ship went on her way; but whether that youth, after they emerged from the heavy oppression of the tropical calms, ever sought for the solution of the old man's statement, remains unknown.

2

I.

The Circle of Blessing.

" Freely ye have received, freely give."

MATTHEW X. S.

"COME back to me, my children—let us not part ;" murmured the Sea to the Vapours, which rose from its surface, drawn upwards by the heat of the tropical sun. " Return to my bosom, and contribute your share to the preservation of my greatness and strength."

" There is no lasting greatness, but in distributed good," replied the Vapours; " behold, we carry your cooling influence to the heated air around. Let us alone, oh Sea ! The work is good."

[14]

"But done at my expense," murmured the Sea. "Is the air your parent, as I am, that you are so careful of its interests? Then why are you so neglectful of mine? Can you afford to be ungrateful to me, from whom your very existence springs? Deluded children! by diminishing my power you are sapping the foundations of your own life. Your very being depends on mine."

"Small and great, great and small, we all depend on each other," sang the Vapours, as they hovered in the air. "Mighty Ocean, give us of your abundance for those that need. It is but little that we ask."

"Divided interests are the ruin of fools," muttered the angry Sea.

"But extended ones the glory of the wise," replied the Vapours, as they still continued to rise. "See, now, have we not done, ourselves, what we would have you also do? Behold, we have left our salts in your bosom for those that need them."

"And I have cast them as a useless burden

to my lowest depths," exclaimed the Sea, indignantly. "Have I not enough, already?
Superfluous bounties deserve but little thanks,
methinks."

"Yet in those depths perchance they may
be welcomed, as we are above," persisted the
Vapours. "It is ever thus: and all will be
made good at last. Small and great, great
and small, we are dependent on each other
evermore."

"Begone, then," moaned the Sea. "You,
who are willing to sacrifice a certain good
for an uncertain conjecture, begone, and be
yourselves the first victims of your folly.
The breezes, that are now driving you forward across my surface, will rise to fury, and
blow you into nothingness as you proceed.
Scattered among the stormy gusts, where
then will be my recompense for your loss?
You, however, will not even exist to repent
of your mad desertion of your home. Adieu!
for ever and for ever, adieu!"

"Adieu, but not for ever," answered the Vapours, as they dispersed before the wind.

It was not a satisfactory parting, perhaps; but often as their race had made the journey round the earth, it had never fallen within the power of any portion of them to explain the course of their career to the surface Sea, which grudged their departure. However, the Vapours had now commenced their circuit, and, carried onward by the steady south-east trade-winds to the regions of equatorial calms, they were met, in that wonderful belt of heat and accumulation, by breezes which in like manner were travelling from the north; and here this meeting caused for a while a lingering in their career. But these opposing winds, laden with vapours from the two hemispheres, had each their mission, and worked under an appointed law.

It was their province to carry the exhalations from north to south into the cooler sky above, where once more their course was free to travel round the world. Ascending thus,

2*

however, when the Vapours entered a more temperate atmosphere, their particles expanded, and a portion of them clung together in drops, which, whilst under the influence of excessive heat, they could never do. They then became much heavier than before ; so heavy, indeed, that the winds were not able to bear them aloft.

"You cannot carry us all," said the Vapours to their struggling supporters. "Some of us will, therefore, return with a message of comfort to the mighty Sea, to tell him all is well."

But even when they came down in torrents of rain to his bosom, the Sea grumbled still. "It is well that a part, at least, of what was lost, returns," said he. But he neither knew nor cared what became of the rest.

The rest, however, fared happily and well : for high above earth and sea—so high, indeed, that they in no way interfered with the winds that swept below—they were borne along by the upper currents of air which were travelling to the north, and carried them forward on their journey of beneficence, and never-ceasing good.

Surely, it must have been a sweet sensation to have been drifted along by a never varying breeze through the higher regions of the sky, undisturbed by care, in a dream of delicious idleness and ease. But this was but a portion of the career of the Vapours from the Sea. At the next meeting, at the outskirts of the tropics, with travellers like themselves coming in the opposite direction, there was a fresh pressure of opposing breezes, a temporary lingering, and then a descent, by which they left those higher regions for ever. Henceforth they were to be dispersed by surface winds on their course of usefulness to man.

And if those Vapours had, for a time. when cradled in that blissful passage high over the tropics, forgotten their mission, there was no possibility of forgetting it henceforth. Taken up with triumphant delight by all the varying breezes that sport over the northern hemisphere, there was no direction in which they were not to be found. A portion was wanted here, another portion there; the snows of Iceland, and the vineyards of Italy, the orange groves of Spain, and the river which pours over the mighty rocks of Niagara, must all be fed at their appointed seasons, and the food was travelling to them now.

But the weary eye looks unsympathizingly round the vast expanse of the globe. It is enough if we can follow the Vapours through some stages of their journey of love.

On the summit of a mountain, over whose sides the gorse and heather were wont to flower together in bright profusion, and with their lovely intermixture of hues, all the ground was parched and dry. A burning sun by day, rarely followed by dewy nights; a summer drought, in fact, had ruled for weeks over the spot, and the shrunken flower-buds and parched leaves bore painful witness to the fact. The little mountain tarn below was almost dry, and the Sundew flowers by its sides, which were wont to revel in the damp surrounding moss, had lost their nature altogether, and never now offered their coronet of sparkling drops to the admiration of those that passed.

The pretty tumbling waterfall lower down, too, which travellers used to delight to visit, and which was fed by streams from the hills, was reduced to a miserable trickle. Cottage children were sent to fetch water from distances so great, that they sat down and wept by the road-side on their errand ; and farmers wore a gloomy, anxious look, which told of a thousand fears about their crops and cattle.

But, while they were thus troubled and careful, lo, the rescue was coming from afar ! yea, travelling towards them upon the wings of the wind. Vapours from tropical seas, Vapours which had left behind them their no-longer-needed salt, were coming, accumulated as clouds, to fall as gracious rain and dews upon the thirsty regions of the North.

They are variable and fantastic winds, perhaps, that course over the northern hemisphere : not steady and uniform in their direction, like the trade-winds in the Tropics ; nor like those upper currents far above the trade-winds, which carry the Vapours to the second belts of calms. No! variable and fantastic they certainly are, and, therefore, we cannot reckon on their arrival to a day,— nay, not to a month ; but on their arrival at last we may always surely depend, and perhaps, in this trial of patient expectation, there is a lesson of quiet faith intended to be learnt.

And so, just as farmers, and cottage children, and the earth and its flowers, and leaves, and springs of water, had all sunk into a state of dismal distrust and discomfort, the deliverance came to them as they slept!

Slight variations in the wind had been observed for more than a day; but still no change of weather took place, until one night a steady breeze from the south-west set in, and prevailed for hours. And presently there was a gathering up of clouds all over the sky, though in the darkness of the night their arrival passed unobserved.

Gracious clouds! they were the Vapours of the Sea, which, after many wanderings, had found their way here, at last, on their mission of love. And, lo! the sound of waters was heard once more on the dried-up hills, and sweet, heavy showers dropped down on the delighted earth. All night long it continued, and all night long the earth was streaming tears of joy; and another day and another night succeeded, during which more or less rain or dew continued to descend.

"Welcome, welcome, O ye showers and dew!" were the Earth's first words; and, "Leave me now no more," her constant after-cry.

"Poor Earth! poor Earth!" murmured the

Vapours, which, condensed into rain-drops, were trembling, like diamonds, on the leaves and flowers in the sunshine of the second dawn. "Poor Earth! poor Earth! you too refuse to learn the law which brought us here. What you have received so freely, will you not freely give?"

"Nay; but linger with me yet," expostulated the Earth; "and let me rather store up the superfluity for future use for myself. What do I know of the future, and what it may bring forth? How can I be sure that the fitful winds will supply me again in time of need? I cannot afford to think of others. Leave me, leave me not.

"None must store against a possible future evil, when so many are suffering under a present one," replied the Vapours; "nevertheless, a message of comfort will come to you, after we are gone."

And so, when the sun shone out in his heat and glory, the diamond rain-drops were drawn upwards from the flowers and leaves into the air once more. Only the little Sun-dews kept their coronets of crystal beads throughout the **day, as** was their custom ; though how they managed it, it would be hard to say.

Perhaps as their own natural juices are so **thick and** clammy, these, mingling with the Vapours **as** they exuded, held them longer fast.

"You are our prisoners," was the trium-phant cry of the Sundew flowers, as they glistened in their liquid gems.

"Nay, but why would you detain us, self-ish flowers?" exclaimed **the Vapours.**

"Oh ! **you** shall **go,** you shall **go ;** but only gradually, as the moisture courses through our veins to re supply your place. This is our way of **life.** But we must hear all from you first. All ! all ! **all !** and most of all, why **you have tarried** so long, till we had almost perished in the dreadful drought ?"

It was a long story the Vapours had then to tell, of their irregular passage to the Polar

Seas ; and how, after their chilly sojourn there as snow, they had passed southwards once more on the summits of drifting icebergs, and again been exhaled, and given back to the ministry of the wandering winds.

"Surely," said they, "we have touched no place in all our wild journeyings where we have not left some blessing behind. Here and there, indeed, folks think they have had too much of us, and here and there too little ; but, oh, my delicate friends, believe us, we are faithful and true to our mission all over the world. Behold, we pour into the earth as rain, or slide into it as moisture ; and lo ! the soil gives its gases into our care, and the roots of the plants draw us and them up together, and, feeding on them, expand, and flourish, and grow ; and when the useful deed is done, and the sun shines down on our labour, up we ascend again to its absorbing rays, to be carried forward again and again, to other gracious deeds. Blame us not, therefore, if, in turning aside to some other case of need, we have come a little late to your hills. Own that you have not been forgotten!"

"It is true," murmured the Sundews, in return; "but remember, we pine and die without your presence."

"Dear little Sundews, there is not a flower in all the boggy heaths that is so dear to us as you are. See, now, we linger with you yet; there is moisture in your mossy bed around this tarn to last for many weeks; and ever as a portion of us steals away, its place shall be supplied from below, so that your flowers shall never miss their sparkling diadem of gems."

The Sundews had no need to tremble after that; but as the exhalations went up from the surface ground, and the moisture sank lower and lower down into it, a fear stole over the Earth that another drought might arise, for she knew not that all would return to her again in due season. But, when in the cool of the evening the Vapours descended upon her bosom, as refreshing mist and dew, she received a portion of comfort. Nevertheless, like the Sea, she grumbled on.

"It is well that a part, at least, of what was lost, returns!" she remarked, in her greedy anxiety, as the sea had done before; and, like him, she neither knew nor cared what became of the rest.

There was a mission for every portion, however; and through the now saturated ground the rain-drops sank together, amidst roots, and stones, and soil, moistening all before them as they went, and replenishing the springs that ran among the hills.

The tumbling Waterfall had, by this time, well nigh given up hope. The mournful trickle with which it fell was an absolute mockery of its former precipitous haste;— when lo! some sudden influence is at work; a rush of vigour flows into the exhausted veins; there is a swelling in the distant springs; nearer and nearer it comes, and now, over the rocky ledge there is a heavier flow; a little more, and yet a little more; and then, at last, a rush of water full and fresh is heard!

"Welcome! welcome! O ye Springs and Floods," cried the Waterfall, as once more it rolled in its beauty along its precipitous course, scattering foam and spray upon the moss and flowers that graced its edge. "Stay in the mountains always, that I may thirst no more; leave me, leave me not again!"

"You, too, who live by giving and receiving," cried the Vapours, as they flushed the stream—"you, too, wishing to stop the gracious course of good? Oh shame, shame, shame!"

And then, as if in mockery of the request, a playful gust blew off from the waterfall as it descended, some of its glittering spray, and tossed it to the sunshiny air, where it dispersed once more in smoky mist,—but only to return in time of need.

Down in the lower country, where stately houses, enclosed in noble parks, adorned the land, a beautiful lake lay stretched under the noon-day sun. It was fed by the stream which, at some miles' distance, received the tumbling waterfall into its course, and then ran through the lake's broad sheet, escaping at the further end in a quick-flowing rill. On the placid, mirror-like surface majestic swans swept proudly by, not unsusceptible of the freshening in the water from the filling of the springs above.

A little pleasure-boat was floating lazily about, impelled occasionally forward by the stroke of an oar from a youth who, with one companion of his own age, and an elderly man who sat abstractedly reading a book, formed the passengers of this tiny bark.

The rower's young companion was lounging in a half-sitting, half-reclining posture in the bows of the boat, and both were gazing at the old Baronial Hall, which, with its quaint turrets, long terraces, and picturesque gardens, faced the lake at a slightly distant elevation, where it stood embosomed in trees.

"Well! if the place were to be mine," ejaculated the lounger, with his eyes fixed upon it, "I know exactly what I should do. I would throw all your agricultural and educational, and endless improvement schemes overboard at once; leave them for those whose business it is to look after them; and enjoy myself, and live like a prince while I had the chance."

"And die worse than a beggar at last," cried the other youth, as he rested on his oars and looked at his cousin who had spoken —"I mean without a friend! You cannot secure even enjoyment, in stagnation," added he. "The very pond here is kept pure by giving out through a stream at one end, what it receives through a stream at the other."

"And the stream from which it receives," said the old man, looking up from his book, "is a type of God Himself; and the stream to which it gives, is a type of the human race. Those who receive from the fountain,

without giving to the stream, work equally
against the laws of Nature and of God."

A few strokes of the oar here carried the
boat away, but surely that was the voice of
him who, in the bygone year, had startled
the ignorant murmurer in the voyage across
the Line! Well is it with those who in the
secrets of Nature read the wisdom of God!

Softly did that summer evening sink upon
the park and the old Baronial Hall, and
heavy were the mists and dews that hung
over the woods, and gardens, and flowers,
and great was the rejoicing in the country
round, when after a time, they were followed
by fertilizing rains. Fertilizing rains!—the
words are easily spoken, but who knows
their full meaning, save him who has watched
over corn-fields or vineyards, threatened with
ill-timed drought? We take a great deal
for granted in this world, and expect that
every thing as a matter of course ought to
fit into our humours, and wishes, and wants;
and it is often only when danger threatens,

that we awake to the discovery, that the guiding reins are held by One whom we had well-nigh forgotten in our careless ease.

"If it had not thundered, the peasant had not made the sign of the cross," is the rude proverb of a distant land ; and peasant and king are alike implicated in its meaning.

"It is all right now," observed the farmer, as he returned home in the evening, after contemplating the goodly acres drenched and dripping with rain.

And it was all right indeed, for, long after the farmer had forgotten his previous anxieties in sleep, the circle of blessing was at work in the length and breadth of his fields.

There, the condensed Vapours sank into the willing soil, which gave to them her gases and her salts. There, the fibres of the roots of corn or grass sucked up the welcome food which brought strength and power into the juices of the plant ; and then, by slow but sure degrees, the stunted ears began to fill, and men said the harvest would be good.

"Stay with us for ever," asked the Corn-ears of the Vapours, as they felt themselves swell under the delicious influence. The Vapours made no answer, for they did not like to speak of death ; but they dealt gently with the corn, and did not leave it till it had ripened gradually for the harvest, and no longer needed their aid ; and then they exhaled once more into the air, to follow out their mission elsewhere.

A curly-headed urchin stood by a pump, looking disconsolately at the huge heavy handle, which he could not lift. A little watering-pot was grasped in his hands, and it was easy to see what he wanted. Some one passing by observed him, and with a smile gave him help. A very few strokes of the handle brought up the water from below, the little watering-pot was filled, and the child ran away. He had a garden of his own ; a garden in which a few kidney-beans in one place, and sweet peas in another, with scatterings of mustard and cress, formed a not very usual mixture ; but it served its purpose of giving employment and pleasure to the child.

The kidney-beans which he hoped to eat at dinner, were evidently the objects of his most attentive care, for he soaked them again and again with the water from his pot. tossing only a few drops of it over the flowers. Little guessed he of the long, long journey the Vapours of the Sea had made before they helped to fill the springs which fed the well over which the pump was built. Little guessed he either of what would become of them when, after helping to fill his kidney-beans with delicate juices, they returned back to the ministry of the winds.

When he touched his pinafore, after he had finished his work, he found it soaked with wet ; and when, soon after, he saw it hung in front of the fire to dry, he sat down and amused himself by watching the steam as it rose from the linen, under the influence of heat.

Trifling it seems to tell—an every-day occurrence of life, not worth a record : yet there was a law even for the vapour that rose from the infant's pinafore in front of the nursery fire. Nothing shall be lost of that which God has ordained to good ; and the Vapours were soon on their mission again. Through the chimney or window they escaped to the cooler air, and returned to their ceaseless work.

" Give us of your salts," was at last their request, as they percolated through the lower ground to join the mighty rivers which ran into the Sea. " Give us of your salts, and lime, and mineral virtues, oh thou Earth! that we may bear them with us to the Sea from which we came."

" Is not the Sea sufficient to itself ?" inquired the jealous Earth.

" None are sufficient to themselves, oh careful Mother !" answered the Vapours, as they streamed in water along their way. "Small and great, great and small, we all depend on each other. How shall the Shells, and Coral Reefs, and Zoöphytes of the deep, continue to grow and live, if you refuse them the virtues of your soil? Give us of your salts, and lime, and the mineral deposites of your bosom, oh Mother Earth! that they may live and rejoice."

"Have you nothing to offer in return?" asked the still-hesitating Earth.

"Do you not know that we have left a blessing behind us wherever we have been?" exclaimed the Vapours. "But no matter for the past. See, we will do ourselves as we would have you do. We will bind ourselves in beauty in the caves of your kingdom, and live with you for ever."

So, as they passed on their way, loading themselves with the virtues of the Earth, some turned aside, and sinking to the subterranean depths, oozed with their limy burden through the roofs of caverns and sides

4

of rocks, and were suspended in graceful stalactites, or shone out in many-sided crystal forms.

"Now I am satisfied," observed the Earth. "What I see I know. They have left me something behind for what they have taken away."

"And now we are satisfied," cried the rest of the Vapours, as they poured into the rivers and were carried out into the Sea. "Have we not returned with a blessing and treasures in our hand?"

And thus, from age to age, ever since the primary mists went up from the earth and watered the whole face of the ground, the mighty work has gone on, and still continues its course. For not to inactivity and idleness did the Vapours now return, but only to recommence afresh their labours of love. Yes! evermore rejoicing on their way, through all varieties of accident, of climate, and of place, whether as Snow or Hail, as Showers or Dews, as Floods or Springs, as

Rivers or as Seas, the waters are still obe-
diently fulfilling His word that called them
into being, and are carrying the everlasting
Circle of Blessing round the world.

Oh, ye showers and dew ; oh, ye winds of
God ; oh, ye ice and snow ; oh, ye seas and
floods ; verily, even when man is mute and
forgetful, ye bless the Lord, ye praise Him
and magnify Him for ever!

II.

A Lesson of Faith.

"If a man die, shall he live *again*? All the days of my appointed time will I wait, till my change come."—JOB xiv. 14.

"LET me hire you as a nurse for my poor children," said a Butterfly to a quiet Caterpillar, who was strolling along a cabbage-leaf in her odd, lumbering way. "See these little eggs," continued the Butterfly; "I don't know how long it will be before they come to life, and I feel very sick and poorly; and if I should die, who will take care of my baby butterflies when I am gone? Will *you*, kind, mild, green Caterpillar? But you must mind what you give them to eat, Caterpillar! —they cannot, of course, live on *your* rough food. You must give them early dew, and

[40]

honey from the flowers; and you must let them fly about only a little way at first; for, of course, one can't. expect them to use their wings properly all at once. Dear me! it is a sad pity you cannot fly yourself. But I have no time to look for another nurse now, so you will do your best, I hope. Dear! dear! I cannot think what made me come and lay my eggs on a cabbage-leaf! What a place for young butterflies to be born upon! Still you will be kind, will you not, to the poor little ones? Here, take this gold-dust from my wings as a reward. Oh, how dizzy I am! Caterpillar! you will remember about the food ——"

And with these words the Butterfly closed her eyes and died; and the green Caterpillar, who had not had the opportunity of even saying Yes or No to the request, was left standing alone by the side of the Butterfly's eggs.

"A pretty nurse she has chosen, indeed, poor lady!" exclaimed she, " and a pretty business I have in hand! Why, her senses must have left her, or she never would have asked a poor crawling creature like me to bring up her dainty little ones! Much they'll mind me, truly, when they feel the gay wings on their backs, and can fly away out of my sight whenever they choose! Ah! how silly some people are, in spite of their painted clothes and the gold-dust on their wings!"

However, the poor Butterfly was dead, and there lay the eggs on the cabbage-leaf; and the green Caterpillar had a kind heart, so she resolved to do her best. But she got no sleep that night, she was so very anxious. She made her back quite ache with walking all night long round her young charges, for fear any harm should happen to them; and in the morning says she to herself—

"Two heads are better than one. I will consult some wise animal upon the matter, and get advice. How should a poor crawling creature like me know what to do, without asking my betters?"

But still there was a difficulty—whom should the Caterpillar consult? There was the shaggy Dog who sometimes came into the garden. But he was so rough!—he would most likely whisk all the eggs off the cabbage-leaf with one brush of his tail, if she should call him near to talk to her, and then she should never forgive herself. There was the Tom Cat, to be sure, who would sometimes sit at the foot of the apple-tree, basking himself and warming his fur in the sunshine; but he was so selfish and indifferent!—there was no hope of his giving himself the trouble to think about butterflies' eggs. "I wonder which is the wisest of all the animals I know," sighed the Caterpillar, in great distress; and then she thought, and thought, till at last she thought of the Lark; and she fancied that because he went up so high, and nobody knew where he went to, he must be very clever, and know a great deal; for to go up very high (which *she* could never do) was the Caterpillar's idea of perfect glory.

Now, in the neighboring corn-field there lived a Lark, and the Caterpillar sent a message to him, to beg him to come and talk to her ; and when he came she told him all her difficulties, and asked him what she was to do to feed and rear the little creatures, so different from herself.

" Perhaps you will be able to inquire and hear something about it next time you go up high," observed the Caterpillar, timidly.

The Lark said, " Perhaps he should ;" but he did not satisfy her curiosity any further. Soon afterwards, however, he went singing upwards into the bright, blue sky. By degrees his voice died away in the distance, till the green Caterpillar could not hear a sound. It is nothing to say she could not see him ; for, poor thing ! she never could see far at any time, and had a difficulty in looking upwards at all, even when she reared herself up most carefully, which she did now ; but it was of no use,—so she dropped upon her legs again, and resumed her walk round the Butterfly's eggs, nibbling a bit of the cabbage-leaf now and then as she moved along.

"What a time the Lark has been gone!" she cried, at last. "I wonder where he is, just now! I would give all my legs to know! He must have flown up higher than usual this time, I do think! How I should like to know where it is that he goes to, and what he hears in that curious blue sky! He always sings in going up and coming down, but he never lets any secret out. He is very, very close!"

And the green Caterpillar took another turn round the Butterfly's eggs.

At last the Lark's voice began to be heard again. The Caterpillar almost jumped for joy, and it was not long before she saw her friend descend with hushed note to the cabbage-bed.

"News, news, glorious news, friend Caterpillar !" sang the Lark; "but the worst of it is, you won't believe me!"

"I believe everything I am told," observed the Caterpillar, hastily.

"Well, then, first of all, I will tell you what these little creatures are to eat"—and the Lark nodded his beak towards the eggs. "What do you think it is to be? Guess!"

"Dew, and the honey out of flowers, I am afraid," sighed the Caterpillar.

"No such thing, old lady! Something simpler than that. Something that *you* can get at quite easily."

"I can get at nothing quite easily but cabbage-leaves," murmured the Caterpillar, in distress.

"Excellent! my good friend," cried the Lark, exultingly; "you have found it out. You are to feed them with cabbage-leaves."

"*Never!*" said the Caterpillar, indignantly. "It was their dying mother's last request that I should do no such thing."

"Their dying mother knew nothing about

the matter," persisted the Lark ; "but why do you ask me, and then disbelieve what I say? You have neither faith nor trust."

" Oh, I believe everything I am told," said the Caterpillar.

" Nay, but you do not," replied the Lark ; " you won't believe me even about the food, and yet that is but a beginning of what I have to tell you. Why, Caterpillar, what do you think those little eggs will turn out to be ? "

" Butterflies, to be sure," said the Caterpillar.

" *Caterpillars !*" sang the Lark ; "and you'll find it out in time ; " and the Lark flew away, for he did not want to stay and contest the point with his friend.

" I thought the Lark had been wise and kind," observed the mild, green Caterpillar, once more beginning to walk round the eggs. "but I find that he is foolish and saucy instead. Perhaps he went up *too* high this time. Ah, it's a pity when people who soar

so high are silly and rude nevertheless!
Dear! I still wonder whom he sees, and
what he does up yonder."

"I would tell you, if you would believe
me," sang the Lark, descending once more.

"I believe everything I am told," reiterated
the Caterpillar, with as grave a face as if it
were a fact.

"Then I'll tell you something else," cried
the Lark; "for the best of my news remains
behind. *You will one day be a Butterfly
yourself.*"

"Wretched bird!" exclaimed the Caterpillar, "you jest with my inferiority—now
you are cruel as well as foolish. Go away!
I will ask your advice no more."

"I told you you would not believe me,"
cried the Lark, nettled in his turn.

"I believe everything that I am told,"
persisted the Caterpillar; "that is"—and
she hesitated,—"everything that it is *reasonable* to believe. But to tell me that butterflies' eggs are caterpillars, and that cater-

pillars leave off crawling and get wings, and become butterflies!——Lark! you are too wise to believe such nonsense yourself, for you know it is impossible."

"I know no such thing," said the Lark, warmly. "Whether I hover over the corn-fields of earth, or go up into the depths of the sky, I see so many wonderful things, I know no reason why there should not be more. Oh, Caterpillar! it is because you crawl, because you never get beyond your cabbage-leaf, that you call *any* thing *impossible*.

"Nonsense!" shouted the Caterpillar; "I know what's possible, and what's not possible, according to my experience and capacity, as well as you do. Look at my long green body and these endless legs, and then talk to me about having wings and a painted, feathery coat! Fool!——"

"And fool you! you would-be-wise Caterpillar!" cried the indignant Lark. "Fool, to attempt to reason about what you cannot understand! Do you not hear how my song swells with rejoicing as I soar upwards to the mysterious wonder-world above? Oh, Caterpillar! what comes to you from there. receive, as *I* do, upon trust."

"That is what you call——"

"*Faith*," interrupted the Lark.

"How am I to learn Faith?" asked the Caterpillar—

At that moment she felt something at her side. She looked round—eight or ten little green caterpillars were moving about, and had already made a show of a hole in the cabbage-leaf. They had broken from the Butterfly's eggs!

Shame and amazement filled our green friend's heart, but joy soon followed; for, as the first wonder was possible, the second might be so too. "Teach me your lesson. Lark!" she would say; and the Lark sang to her of the wonders of the earth below. and of the heaven above. And the Caterpillar talked all the rest of her life, to her relations, of the time when she should be a Butterfly.

But none of them believed her. She nevertheless had learnt the Lark's lesson of faith, and when she was going into her chrysalis grave, she said—"I shall be a butterfly some day !"

But her relations thought her head was wandering, and they said, "Poor thing !"

And when she was a Butterfly, and was going to die again, she said—

"I have known many wonders—I have faith—I can trust even now for what shall come next !"

III.

The Law of Authority and Obedience.

" Who made thee a ruler and a judge over us ? "

ACTS vii. 27.

A FINE young Working-bee left his hive, one lovely summer's morning, to gather honey from the flowers. The sun shone so brightly, and the air felt so warm, that he flew a long, long distance, till he came to some gardens that were very beautiful and gay ; and there, having roamed about, in and out of the flowers, buzzing in great delight, till he had so loaded himself with treasures that he could carry no more, he bethought himself of returning home. But, just as he was beginning his journey, he accidentally flew through the open window of a country house, and

[52]

found himself in a large dining-room. There was a great deal of noise and confusion, for it was dinner-time, and the guests were talking rather loudly, so that the Bee got quite frightened. Still he tried to taste some rich sweetmeats that lay temptingly in a dish on the table, when all at once he heard a child exclaim with a shout, " Oh, there's a bee ; let me catch him !" on which he rushed hastily back to (as he thought) the open air. But, alas! poor fellow, in another second he found that he had flung himself against a hard, transparent wall ! In other words, he had flown against the glass panes of the window, being quite unable, in his alarm and confusion, to distinguish the glass from the opening by which he had entered. This unexpected blow annoyed him much ; and having wearied himself in vain attempts to find the entrance he began to walk slowly and quietly up and down the wooden frame at the bottom of the panes, hoping to recover both his strength and composure.

5*

Presently, as he was walking along, his attention was attracted by hearing the soft, half-whispering voices of two children, who were kneeling down and looking at him.

Says the one to the other, "This is a working-bee, Sister ; I see the wax-bags under his thighs. Nice fellow ! how busy he has been !"

"Does he make the wax and honey himself?" whispered the Girl.

"Yes, he gets them from the insides of the flowers. Don't you remember how we watched the bees once dodging in and out of the crocuses, how we laughed at them, they were so busy and fussy, and their dark coats looked so handsome against the yellow leaves ? I wish I had seen this fellow loading himself to-day. But he does more than that. He builds the honeycomb, and does pretty nearly everything. He's a working-bee, poor wretch ! "

" What is a working-bee ? and why do you call him 'Poor wretch,' Brother ?"

"Why, don't you know, Uncle Collins

says all people are poor wretches who work for other people who don't work for themselves? And that is just what this bee does. There is the queen-bee in the hive, who does nothing at all but sit at home, give orders, and coddle the little ones ; and all the bees wait upon her, and obey her. Then there are the drones—lazy fellows, who lounge all their time away. And then there are the working-bees, like this one here, and they do all the work for everybody. How Uncle Collins would laugh at them, if he knew !"

"Doesn't Uncle Collins know about bees?"

"No, I think not. It was the gardener who told me. And, besides, I think Uncle Collins would never have done talking about them and quizzing them, if he once knew they couldn't do without a queen. I heard him say, yesterday, that kings and queens were against nature, for that nature never makes one man a king and another man a cobbler, but makes them all alike ; and so, he says, kings and queens are very unjust things."

" Bees have not the sense to know any-thing about that," observed the little Girl, softly.

" Of course not!   Only fancy how angry these working fellows would be, if they knew what the gardener told me ! "

" What was that ? "

" Why, that the working-bees are just the same as the queen when they are first born, just exactly the same, and that it is only the food that is given them, and the shape of the house they live in, that makes the difference. The bee-nurses manage that ; they give some one sort of food, and some another, and they make the cells different shapes ; and so some turn out queens, and the rest working-bees. It's just what Uncle Collins says about kings and cobblers—nature makes them all alike. But, look ! the dinner's over ; we must go."

" Wait till I let the Bee out, Brother," said the little Girl, taking him gently up in a soft handkerchief ; and then she looked at him kindly, and said, "Poor fellow ! so you might have been a queen if they had only given you the right food, and put you into a right-shaped house! What a shame they didn't! As it is, my good friend," (and here her voice took a childish, mocking tone)— "As it is, my good friend, you must go and drudge away all your life long, making honey and wax. Well, get along with you! Good luck to your labours!" And with these words she fluttered her handkerchief through the open window, and the Bee found himself once more floating in the air.

Oh, what a fine evening it was! But the liberated Bee did not think so. The sun still shone beautifully, though lower in the sky; and though the light was softer, and the shadows were longer; and as to the flowers, they were more fragrant than ever; yet the poor Bee felt as if there were a dark, heavy cloud over the sky; but in reality the cloud was over his own heart, for he had become discontented and ambitious, and he rebelled against the authority under which he had been born.

At last he reached his home—the hive which he had left with such a happy heart in the morning—and, after dashing in, in a hurried and angry manner, he began to unload the bags under his thighs of their precious contents, and as he did so he exclaimed, "I am the most wretched of creatures!"

"What is the matter? what have you done?" cried an old Relation who was at work near him; "have you been eating the poisonous kalmia flowers, or have you discovered that the mischievous honey-moth has laid her eggs in our combs?"

"Oh, neither, neither!" answered the Bee, impatiently; "only I have travelled a long way, and have heard a great deal about myself that I never knew before, and I know now that we are a set of wretched creatures!"

"And, pray, what wise animal has been

persuading you of that, against your own experience?" asked the old Relation.

"I have learnt *a truth*," answered the Bee, in an indignant tone, "and it matters not who taught it me."

"Certainly not; but it matters very much that you should not fancy yourself wretched merely because some foolish creature has told you you are so; you know very well that you never *were* wretched till you were told you were so. I call that very silly; but I shall say no more to you." And the old Relation turned himself round to his work, singing very pleasantly all the time.

But the Traveller-bee would not be laughed out of his wretchedness: so he collected some of his young companions around him, and told them what he had heard in the large dining-room of the country-house; and all were astonished, and most of them vexed. Then he grew so much pleased at finding himself able to create such excitement and interest, that he became sillier every minute, and made a long speech on the injustice of there being such things as queens, and talked of nature making them all equal and alike, with an energy that would have delighted Uncle Collins himself.

When the Bee had finished his speech, there was first a silence, and then a few buzzes of anger, and then a murmured expression of plans and wishes. It must be admitted their ideas of how to remedy the evil now for the first time suggested to them were very confused. Some wished Uncle Collins could come and manage all the bee-hives in the country, for they were sure he would let *all* the bees be queens, and then what a jolly time they should have! And when the old Relation popped his head round the corner of the cell he was building, just to inquire, " What would be the fun of being queens, if there were no working-bees to wait on one?" the little coterie of rebels buzzed very loud, and told him he was a fool, for of course Uncle Collins would take care

that the tyrant who had so long been queen.
and the royal children, now ripening in their
nurse-cells, should be made to wait on them
while they lasted.

"And when they are finished?" persisted
the old Relation, with a laugh.

"Buzz, buzz," was the answer; and the old
Relation held his tongue.

Then another Bee suggested that it would.
after all, be very awkward for them all to
be queens; for who would make the honey
and wax, and build the honeycombs, and
nurse the children? Would it not be best,
therefore, that there should be no queens
whatever, but that they should all be working-bees?

But then the tiresome old Relation popped
his head round the corner again, and said, he
did not quite see how that change would
benefit them, for were they not all working-
bees already?—on which an indignant buzz
was poured into his ear, and he retreated
again to his work.

6

It was well that night at last came on, and
the time arrived when the labours of the day
were over, and sleep and silence must reign
in the hive. With the dawn of the morning,
however, the troubled thoughts unluckily returned, and the Traveller-bee and his companions kept occasionally clustering together
in little groups, to talk over their wrongs
and a remedy. Meantime, the rest of the
hive were too busy to pay much attention to
them, and so their idleness was not detected.
But, at last, a few hot-headed youngsters
grew so violent in their different opinions,
that they lost all self-control, and a noisy
quarrel would have broken out, but that the
Traveller-bee flew to them, and suggested
that, as they were grown up now, and could
not all be turned into queens, they had best
sally forth and try the republican experiment
of all being working-bees without any queen
whatever. With so charming an idea in
view, he easily persuaded them to leave the
hive ; and a very nice swarm they looked as

they emerged into the open air, and dispersed
about the garden to enjoy the early breeze.
But a swarm of bees, without a queen to lead
them, proved only a helpless crowd, after all.
The first thing they attempted, when they
had re-collected to consult, was, to fix on the
sort of place in which they should settle for
a home.

"A garden, of course," says one. "A
field," says another. "There is nothing like
a hollow tree," remarked a third. "The
roof of a good outhouse is best protected
from wet," thought a fourth. "The branch
of a tree leaves us most at liberty," cried a
fifth. "I won't give up to anybody," shouted
all.

They were in a prosperous way to settle,
were they not?

"I am very angry with you," cried the
Traveller-bee, at last; "half the morning is
gone already, and here we are as unsettled
as when we left the hive!"

"One would think you were going to be

queen over us, to hear you talk," exclaimed the disputants. "If we choose to spend our time in quarrelling, what is that to you? Go and do as you please yourself!"

And he did; for he was ashamed and unhappy; and he flew to the further extremity of the garden to hide his vexation; where, seeing a clump of beautiful jonquils, he dived at once into a flower to soothe himself by honey-gathering. Oh, how he enjoyed it! He loved the flowers and the honey-gathering more than ever, and began his accustomed murmur of delight, and had serious thoughts of going back at once to the hive as usual, when, as he was coming out of one of the golden cups, he met his old Relation coming out of another.

"Who would have thought to find you here alone?" said the old Relation. "Where are your companions?"

"I scarcely know; I left them outside the garden."

"What are they doing?

" . . . Quarrelling . . ." murmured the
Traveller-bee.

" What about ?"

" What they are to do."

" What a pleasant occupation for bees on
a sunshiny morning !" said the old Relation,
with a sly expression.

" Don't laugh at me, but tell me what to
do," said the puzzled Traveller. " What
Uncle Collins says about nature and our all
being alike, sounds very true, and yet somehow we do nothing but quarrel when we try
to be all alike and equal."

" How old are you ?" asked the old Relation.

" Seven days," answered the Traveller, in
all the sauciness of youth and strength.

" And how old am I ?"

" Many months, I am afraid."

" You are right, I am an oldish bee. Now,
my dear friend, let us fight !"

" Not for the world. I am the stronger,
and should hurt you."

"I wonder what makes you ask advice of a creature so much weaker than yourself?"

"Oh, what can your weakness have to do with your wisdom, my good old Relation? I consult you because I know you are wise; and I am humbled myself, and feel that I am foolish."

"Old and young—strong and weak—wise and foolish—what has become of our being alike and equal? But never mind, we can manage. Now let us agree to live together."

"With all my heart. But where shall we live?"

"Tell me first which of us is to decide, if we differ in opinion?"

"*You* shall; for you are wise."

"Good! And who shall collect honey for food?"

"*I* will; for I am strong."

"Very well; and now you have made me a queen, and yourself a working-bee! Ah! you foolish fellow, won't the old home and the old queen do? Don't you see that if even *two* people live together, there must be a head to lead and hands to follow? How much more in the case of a multitude!"

Gay was the song of the Traveller-bee as he wheeled over the flowers, joyously assenting to the truth of what he heard.

" Now to my companions," he cried, at last. And the two flew away together and sought the knot of discontented youngsters outside the garden wall.

They were still quarrelling, but no energy was left them. They were hungry and confused, and **many** had already flown away, to work and go home as usual.

And **very soon** afterwards a cluster of happy, buzzing bees, headed by the old Relation and the Traveller, were seen returning with wax-laden thighs to their hive.

As they were going to enter, they were stopped by one of the little sentinels who watch the doorway.

" Wait," cried he ; " a royal corpse is ing out !"

And so it was ;—a dead queen soon appeared in sight, dragged along by working-
bees on each side who, having borne her
to the edge of the hive-stand, threw her over
for interment.

"How is this? what has happened?" asked
the Traveller-bee, in a tone of deep anxiety
and emotion : " Surely our queen is not
dead ?"

"Oh, no!" answered the sentinel ; " but
there has been some accidental confusion in the
hive this morning. Some of the cell-keepers
were unluckily absent, and a young queen-
bee burst through her cell, which ought to
have been blocked up for a few days longer.
Of course the two queens fought till one was
dead ; and, of course, the weaker one was
killed. We shall not be able to send off a
swarm quite so soon as usual this year ; but
these accidents can't be helped."

"But this one might have been helped,"
foolisht the Traveller-bee to himself, as with
old queeremorse he remembered that he had

been the cause of the mischievous confusion.

" You see," buzzed the old Relation, nudg-
ing up against him,—" You see even *queens
are not equal!* and that there can be but one
ruler at once !"

And the Traveller-bee murmured a heart-
wrung " Yes."

—And thus the instincts of nature confirm
the reasoning conclusions of man.

IV.

The Unknown Land.

" But now they desire a better country."
HEBREWS xi. 16.

T mattered not to the Sedge Warbler whether it were night or day!

She built her nest down among the willows, and reeds, and long, thick herbage that bordered the great river's side, and in her sheltered covert she sang songs of mirth and rejoicing both by day and night.

"Where does the great river go to?" asked the little ones, as they peered out of their nest one lovely summer night, and saw the moonbeams dancing on the waters, as they hurried along. Now, the Sedge Warbler could not tell her children where the great

[70]

[THE SERGE WARBLERS NEST.]

THE UNKNOWN LAND.

Circle of Blessing.

river went to ; so she laughed, and said they
must ask the Sparrow who chattered so fast,
or the Swallow who travelled so far, next
time one or the other came to perch on the
willow-tree to rest. " And then," said she,
" you will hear all such stories as these !"—
and thereupon the Sedge Warbler tuned
her voice to the Sparrow's note, and the little
ones almost thought the Sparrow was there,
the song was so like his—all about towns,
and houses, and gardens, and fruit-trees, and
cats, and guns ; only the Sedge Warbler
made the account quite confused, for she
had never had the patience to sit and listen
to the Sparrow so as really to understand
what he said about these matters.

But imperfect as the tale was, it amused the
little ones very much, and they tried then to
sing like it, and sang till they fell asleep ;
and when they awoke they burst into singing again ; for, behold ! the eastern sky was
red with the dawn, and they knew the warm
sunbeams would soon send beautiful streaks

of light in among the reeds and flags that sheltered their happy home.

Now, the Mother-bird would sometimes leave the little ones below, and go up into the willow-branches to sing alone ; and as the season advanced she did this oftener and oftener ; and her song was plaintive and tender, then, for she used to sing to the tide of the river, as it swept along she knew not whither, and think that some day she and her husband and children should all be hurrying so onward as the river hurried,—she knew not whither also,—to the Unknown Land whence she had come. Yes! I may call it the Unknown Land ; for only faint images remained upon her mind of the country whence she had flown.

At first she used to sing these ditties only when alone ; but by degrees she began to let her little ones hear them, now and then,—for were they not going to accompany her? and was it not as well, therefore, to accustom them gradually to think about it?

Then the little ones asked her where the said Unknown Land was. But she smiled and she could not tell them, for she did not know.

"Perhaps the great river is travelling there all along," thought the eldest child. But he was wrong. The great river was rolling on hurriedly to a mighty city, where it was to stream through the arches of many bridges, and bear on its bosom the traffic of many nations ; restless and crowded by day ; gloomy, dark, and dangerous by night ! Ah ! what a contrast were the day and night of the mighty city, to the day and night of the Sedge Warbler's home, where the twenty-four hours of changes God has appointed to nature were but so many changes of beauty !

"Mother, why do you sing songs about another land ?" asked a young, tender-hearted fledgling one day. "Why should we leave the reed-beds and the willow-trees ? Can not we all build nests here, and live here always ? Mother, do not let us go away anywhere else. I want no other land, and no other home but

7

this. There are all the aits in the great river to choose from, where we shall each settle; there can be nothing in the Unknown Land more pleasant than the reed-beds and the willow-trees here. I am so happy!—Leave off those dreadful songs!"

Then the Mother's breast heaved with many a varied thought, and she made no reply. So the little one went on,—

" Think of the red glow in the morning sky. Mother, and the soft haze—and then the beautiful rays of warm light across the waters! Think of the grand noonday glare. when the broad flags and reeds are all burnished over with heat. Think of these evenings, Mother, when we can sit about in the branches—here, there, anywhere—and watch the great sun go down behind the sky ; or fly to the aits of the great river, and sing in the long green herbage there ; and then come home by moonlight, and sing till we fall asleep ; and wake singing again, if any noise disturb us. if a boat chance to paddle by, or

some of those strange bright lights shoot up
with a noise into the sky from distant gardens. Think, even when the rain comes
down, how we enjoy ourselves ; for then how
sweet it is to huddle into the soft warm nest
together, and listen to the drops pattering
upon the flags and leaves overhead! Oh! I
love this dear, dear home so much!—Sing
those dreadful songs about another land no
more!"

Then the Mother said—

"Listen to me, my child, and I will sing
you another song."

And the Sedge Warbler changed her note,
and sang to her tender little one of her own
young days, when she was as happy and as gay
as now, though not here among the reed-
beds ; and how, after she had lived and re-
joiced in her happiness many pleasant months,
a voice seemed to rise within her that said—
"*This is not your Rest!*" and how she wondered, and tried not to listen, and tried to
stop where she was, and be happy there still.

But the voice came oftener and oftener, and louder and louder ; and how the dear partner she had chosen heard and felt the same ; and how at last they left their home together, and came and settled down among the reed-beds of the great river ; and oh! how happy she had been !

"And where is the place you came from, Mother?" asked the little one. "Is it anywhere near, that we may go and see it?"

"My child," answered the Sedge Warbler, "it is the Unknown Land! Far, far away, I know ; but *where*, I do not know. Only the voice that called me thence is beginning to call again. And, as I was obedient and hopeful once, shall I be less obedient and hopeful now—now that I have been so happy? No, my little one ; let us go forth to the Unknown Land, wherever it may be, in joyful trust.

"*You* will be with me ; so I will," murmured the little Sedge Warbler in reply ; and before she went to sleep she joined her young voice with her mother's in the Song of the Unknown Land.

One day afterwards, when the parent birds had gone off to the sedgy banks of a neighbouring stream, another of the young ones flew to the topmost branches of some willow-trees, and, delighted with his position, began to sing merrily, as he swung backwards and forwards on a bough. Many were the songs he tried, and well enough he succeeded, for his age ; and at last he tried the song of the Unknown Land.

" A pretty tune, and a pretty voice, and a pretty singer !" remarked a Magpie, who unluckily was crossing the country at the time, and whose mischievous spirit made him stop to amuse himself, by showing off to the young one his superior wisdom, as he thought it.

"I have been in many places, and even once was domesticated about the house of a human creature, so that I am a pretty good judge of singing," continued Mr. Mag, with a cock of his tail, as he balanced himself on

7*

a branch near the Sedge Warbler ; " but, upon my word, I have seldom heard a prettier song than yours—only I wish you would tell me what it is all about."

" It is about the Unknown Land," answered the young Warbler, with modest pleasure, and very innocently.

" Do I hear you right, my little friend ?" inquired the Magpie, with mock solemnity— " The *Unknown* Land, did you say ? Dear, dear ! to think of finding such abstruse philosophy among the marshes and ditches ! It is quite a treat ! And pray, now, what is there that you can tell an old fellow like me, who am always anxious to improve myself, about this Unknown Land ?"

" I don't know, except that we are going there some day," answered the Sedge Warbler, rather confused by the Magpie's manner.

" Now, that is excellent !" returned the Magpie, chuckling with laughter. " How I love simplicity ! and, really, you are a choice specimen of it, Mr. Sedge Warbler. So you

are thinking of a journey to this Unknown
Land, always supposing, of course, my sweet
little friend, that you can find the way to it,
which, between you and me, I think there
must naturally be some doubt about, under
the circumstances of the place itself being
unknown! Good evening to you, pretty Mr.
Sedge Warbler. I wish you a pleasant jour
ney!"

"Oh, stop, stop!" cried the young bird,
now quite distressed by the Magpie's ridicule; "don't go just yet, pray. Tell me
what you think yourself about the Unknown
Land."

"Oh, you little wiseacre, are you laughing
at me? Why, what can *any*body, even so
clever a creature as yourself, *think* about an
unknown thing? You can *guess*, I admit,
anything you please about it, and so could I,
if I thought it worth while to waste my time
so foolishly. But you will never get beyond
guessing in such a case—at all events, I con-

fess *my* poor abilities can't pretend to do anything more."

"Then you are not going there yourself?" murmured the overpowered youngster.

" Certainly not. In the first place, I am quite contented where I am ; and, in the second place, I am not quite so easy of belief as you seem to be. How do I know there is such a place as this Unknown Land at all ?"

" My father and mother told me that," answered the Sedge Warbler, with more confidence.

" Oh, your father and mother told you, did they ?" sneered the Magpie, scornfully. "And you're a good little bird, and believe every-thing your father and mother tell you. And if they were to tell you you were going to live up in the moon, you would believe them, I suppose ?"

" They never deceived me yet !" cried the young Sedge Warbler, firmly, his feathers ruffling with indignation as he spoke.

"Hoity, toity! what's the matter now, my dainty little cock? Who said your father and mother *had* ever deceived you? But, without being a bit *deceitful,* I take the liberty to inform you that they may be extremely *ignorant.* And I shall leave you to decide which of the two, yourself; for, I declare, one gets nothing but annoyance by trying to be good-natured to you countrified young fellows. You are not fit to converse with a bird of any experience and wisdom. So, once for all, good-bye to you!"

And the Magpie flapped his wings, and was gone before the Sedge Warbler had half recovered from his fit of vexation.

There was a decided change in the weather that evening, for the summer was now far advanced, and a sudden storm had brought cooler breezes and more rain than usual; and the young birds wondered, and were sad, when they saw the dark sky, and the swollen river, and felt that there was no warm sunshine to dry the wet, as was usual after a mid-day shower.

" Why is the sky so cloudy and lowering, and why is the river so thick and gloomy, and why is there no sunshine, I wonder ?" says one.

" The sun will shine again to-morrow, I dare say," was the mother's answer; " but the days are shortening fast, and the storm has made this one very short ; and the sun will not get through the clouds this evening. Never mind ! the wet has not hurt the inside of our nest. Get into it my dear ones, and keep warm, while I sing to you about our journey. Silly children, did you expect the sunshine to last here forever ?"

" I hoped it might, and thought it would, once, but lately I have seen a change," answered the young one who had talked to her mother so much before. "And I do not mind now, Mother. When the sunshine goes, and the wet comes, and the river looks dark and the sky black, I think about the Unknown Land."

Then the Mother was pleased, and, perched upon a tall flag outside the nest, she sang a hopeful song of the Unknown Land ; and the father and children joined—all but *one !* He, poor fellow, would not, could not sing ; but when the voices ceased, he murmured to his brothers and sisters in the nest—

" This would be all very pleasant and nice. if we could *know* anything about the Land we talk about."

"If we were to know too much, perhaps we should never be satisfied here," laughed the tender little one, who had formerly been so much distressed about going.

" But we know *nothing,* "rejoined the other bird ; " indeed, how do we know there is such a place as the Unknown Land at all ? "

" We *feel* that there is, at any rate," answered the Sister-bird. " *I* have heard the call our mother tells about, and so must *you* have done."

" You fancy you have heard it, that is to say," cried the Brother ; " because she told you. It is all fancy, all guess-work ; no knowledge ! I could fancy I heard it too, only I will not be so weak and silly ; I will neither think about going, nor will I go."

" *This is not your Rest*," sang the Mother, in a loud, clear voice, outside ; and " *This is not your Rest*," echoed the others in sweet unison ; and " *This is not your Rest*," sounded in the depths of the poor little Sedge Warbler's own heart.

" This is not our Rest ! " repeated the Mother. " The river is rushing forward ; the clouds are hurrying onward ; the winds are sweeping past, because here is not their Rest. Ask the river, ask the clouds, ask the winds where they go to :—Another Land ! Ask the great sun, as he descends away out of sight, where he goes to :—Another Land ! And when the appointed time shall come, let us also arise and go hence."

" O Mother, Mother, would that I could

believe you! Where is that other Land?"
Thus cried the distressed doubter in the nest.
And then he opened his troubled heart, and
told what the Magpie had said, and the
parent birds listened in silence ; and when he
ceased—

"Listen to me, my son," exclaimed the
Mother, " and I will sing you another song."

Whereupon she spoke once more of the
land she had left before ; but now the burden
of her story was, that she had left it *without
knowing why*. She " went out not knowing
whither,"—in blind obedience, faith, and
hope. As she traversed the wide waste of
waters, there was no one to give her *reasons*
for her flight, or tell her, " This and this will
be your lot." Could the Magpie have told
her, had he met her there? But had she
been deceived? **No!** The secret voice
which had called and led her forth, had been
one of Kindness. When she came to the reed-
beds she knew all about it. For then arose
the strong desire to settle. Then she and

8

her dear partner lived together. And then came the thought that she must build a nest. Ah! had the Magpie seen her then, building a home for children yet unborn, how he would have mocked at her! What could she *know*, he would have asked, about the future? Was it not all *guess-work*, fancy, folly? But had she been deceived? No! It was that voice of Kindness that had told her what to do. For did she not become the happy mother of children? And was she not now able to comfort and advise her little ones in their troubles? For, let the Magpie say what he would, was it likely that the voice of Kindness would deceive them at last? "No!" cried she; "in joyful trust let us obey the call, though now we know not why. When obedience and faith are made perfect, it may be that knowledge and explanation shall be given." So ended the Mother's strain, and no sad misgivings ever clouded the Sedge Warbler's home again.

Several weeks of changing autumn weather

followed after this, and the chilly mornings and evenings caused the songs of departure to sound louder and more cheerily than ever in the reed-beds. They knew, they felt, they had confidence, that there was joy for them in the Unknown Land. But one dark morning, when all were busy in various directions, a sudden loud sound startled the young ones from their sports, and in terror and confusion they hurried home. The old nest looked looser and more untidy than ever that day, for some water had oozed in through the half-worn bottom. But they huddled together into it, as of old, for safety. Soon, however, it was discovered that neither Father nor Mother was there ; and after waiting in vain some time for their return, the frightened young ones flew off again to seek them.

Oh! weary, weary search for the missing ones we love ! It may be doubted whether the sad reality, when they came upon it, exceeded the agony of that hour's suspense.

It ended, however, at last! On a patch of long rank herbage which covered a mud bank, so wet that the cruel sportsman could not follow to secure his prey, lay the stricken parent birds. One was already dead ; but the mother still lived, and as her children's wail of sorrow sounded in her ear, she murmured out a last gentle strain of hope, and comfort.

"Away, away, my darlings, to the Unknown Land. The voice that has called to all our race before, and never but for kindness, is calling to you now. Obey! Go forth in joyful trust! Quick! Quick ! There's no time to be lost!"

" But my Father—you—oh, my Mother ! " cried the young ones.

" Hush, sweet ones, hush! We cannot be with you *there*. But there may be some other Unknown Land which *this* may lead to ;" and the Mother laid her head against her wounded side and died.

Long before the sunbeams could pierce the

heavy haze of the next autumn morning, the young Sedge Warblers rose for the last time o'er their much-loved reed-beds, and took flight—" they knew not whither."

Dim and undefined hope, perhaps they had, that they might find their parents again in the Unknown Land. And if one pang of grief struck them when these hopes ended, it was but for a moment; for said the Brother-bird—

" There *may* be some other Unknown Land, better even than this, to which they may be gone."

18*

V.

Knowledge not the Limit of Belief.

INTRODUCTORY NOTE.

ZOÖPHYTES AND CORALLINES.

ALMOST everybody knows what a sea-weed is, but many people may not know that the graceful buff-coloured pieces they pick up among their favourite pink and green specimens are not really sea-weeds, or any sort of *plants*, but *animal creatures*, which are known among Naturalists by the name of ZOÖPHYTES.

They look so like plants, however, to the naked eye, that they were always supposed to be so, until, by being examined through a microscope, it was discovered that these so-

[90]

called plants were covered over with cells, in which tiny live creatures were fixed, and from which they were seen to put out feelers for the purpose of catching prey for food.

But as the tiny creatures (called Polypes) cannot leave their cell-like homes, a Zoöphyte may well be called a compound animal. It is like a shrub, only with animal instead of vegetable sap in all its branches, and a living creature growing in every bud.

CORALLINES are the common lilac-coloured sea-weeds, with a hard limy coating, which are picked up on all our shores, and are well known by sight, if not by name, to all sea-weed gatherers.

The only curious part of their history is, that for more than half a century they were supposed to be animals! This strange mistake was originated by the same distinguished Naturalist, Mr. John Ellis, a London merchant, who first asserted in England the animal nature of the Zoöphytes. And as his statements about them proved to be no less

true than interesting, people took for granted
the correctness of what he said about the
Corallines.   But, within the last few years,
Ellis' mistake began to be suspected ; and
one of the most eminent observers of our own
day, Dr. Johnston, of Berwick, published in
1842 a " History of British Sponges and
Lithophytes," in which this question was set
at rest forever, and their vegetable nature
was proved by the results of the closest examination and the most conclusive experiments.

"Canst thou by searching find out God?"

JOB xi. 7.

T was but the banging of the door, blown to by a current of wind from the open window, that made that great noise, and shook the room so much!

The room was a Naturalist's library, and it was a pity that some folio books of specimens had been left so near the edge of the great table,—for, when the door clapt to, they fell down, and many plants, seaweeds, &c., were scattered on the floor.

And, "Do we meet once again?" said a Zoöphyte to a Seaweed (a *Coralline*) in whose company he had been thrown ashore,—"Do we meet once again? This is a real pleasure. What strange adventures we have

[93]

gone through since the waves flung us on the sands together !"

"Ay, indeed," replied the Seaweed, "and what a queer place we have come to at last! Well, well—but let me first ask you how you are this morning, after all the washing, and drying, and squeezing, and gumming, we have undergone ?"

"Oh, pretty well in health, Seaweed, but very, very sad. You know there is a great difference between you and me. You have little or no cause to be sad. You are just the same now that you ever were, excepting that you can never grow any more. But *I!* ah, I am only the skeleton of what I once was! All the merry little creatures that inhabited me are dead and dried up. They died by hundreds at a time, soon after I left the sea ; and even if they had survived longer, the nasty fresh water we were soaked in by the horrid being who picked us up, would have killed them at once. What are you smiling at ?"

"I am smiling," said the Seaweed, "at your calling our new master a horrid being, and also at your speaking so positively about the little creatures that inhabited you."

"And why may I not speak positively of what I know so well?" asked the other.

"Oh, of what you *know*, Zoöphyte, by all means! But I wonder what we *do* know! People get very obstinate over what they think they know, and then, lo and behold! it turns out to be a mistake."

"What makes you say this?" inquired the Zoöphyte; and the Seaweed answered, "I have learnt it from a very curious creature I have made acquaintance with here—a Book-worm. He walks through all the books in this library just as he pleases, and picks up a quantity of information, and knows a great deal. And he's a mere nothing, he says, compared to the creature who picked us up —the 'horrid being,' as you call him. Why, my dear friend, the Bookworm tells me that he who found us is a man, and that a man is

the most wonderful creature in all the world ;
that there is nothing in the least like him.
And this particular one here is a Naturalist ;
that is, he knows all about living creatures,
and plants, and stones, and I don't know
what besides. Now, wouldn't you say that
it was a great honour to belong to him, and
to have made acquaintance with his friend
the Bookworm ?"

"Of course I should, and do—" the Zoöphyte replied.

"Very well," continued his companion, " I
know you would ; and yet I can tell you that
this Naturalist and his Bookworm are just
instances of what I have been saying. They
fancy that betwixt them they know nearly
everything, and get as obstinate as possible
over the most ridiculous mistakes."

" My good friend Seaweed, are you a com-
petent judge in such matters as these ?"

" Oh, am I not ! " the Seaweed rejoined.
"Why now, for instance, what do you think
the Book-worm and I have been quarrelling

about half the morning? Actually as to whether *I* am an animal or a vegetable. He declares that I am an animal full of little living creatures like yours, and that there is a long account of all this written on the page opposite the one on which I am gummed!"

"Of all the nonsense I ever listened to!" began the Zoöphyte, angrily, yet amused— but he was interrupted by the Seaweed—

"And as for *you*—I am almost ashamed to, tell you--that you and all your family and connections **were**, for generations and generations, considered as vegetables. It is only lately that these Naturalists found out that you were an animal. May I not well say that people get very obstinate about what they think they know, and after all it turns out **to** be a mistake? As for me, I am quite confused with these blunders."

"Oh dear, how disappointed I am!" murmured the Zoöphyte. "I thought we had really fallen into the hands of some very interesting creatures. I am very, very sorry!

9

It seemed so nice that there should be wonderful, wise beings, who spend their time in
finding out all about animals, and plants, and
such things, and keep us all in these beautiful
books so carefully. I liked it so much, and
now I find the wonderfully wise creatures
are wonderfully stupid ones instead."

"Very much so," laughed the Seaweed,
" though our learned friend, the Bookworm,
would tell you quite otherwise ; but he gets
quite muddled when he talks about them,
poor fellow ! "

"It is very easy to ridicule your betters,"
said a strange voice ; and the Bookworm,
who had just then eaten his way through the
back of Lord Bacon's *Advancement of Learning*, appeared sitting outside, listening to the
conversation. "I shall be sorry that I have
told you anything, if you make such a bad
use of the little bit of knowledge you have
acquired."

"Oh, I beg your pardon, dear friend !"
cried the Seaweed. "I meant no harm. You

see it is quite new to us to learn anything ; and, really, if I laughed, you must excuse me. I meant no harm—only I *do* happen to know —really for a fact—that I never was alive with little creatures like my friend the Zoö- phyte, and he happens to know—really for a fact—that he never was a vegetable, and so you see it made us smile to think of your wonderful creature, man, making such won- derfully odd mistakes."

At this the **Bookworm smiled** ; but he soon shook his **head gravely, and** said—"All the mistakes man makes, man can discover and correct—I mean, of course, all the mistakes he makes about creatures inferior to himself, whom he learns to know from his own obser- vation. He may not observe quite carefully enough **one day, but he** may put **all** right when he looks next time. I never give up a statement when I know it is true : and so I tell you again—laugh as much as you please —that, in spite of all his mistakes, man is, without exception, the most wonderful and the most clever of all the creatures upon earth !"

" You will be a clever creature yourself if you can prove it ! " cried both the Zoöphyte and Seaweed at once.

" The idea of taking me with my hundreds of living inhabitants for a vegetable !" sneered the Zoöphyte.

" And me with my vegetable inside, covered over with lime, for an animal ! " smiled the Seaweed.

Bookworm. "Ah ! have your laugh out, and then listen. But, my good friends, if you had worked your way through as many wise books as I have done, you would laugh less and know more."

Zoöphyte. " Nay, don't be angry, Book-worm."

Bookworm. " Oh, I'm not angry a bit. I know too well the cause of all the folly you are talking, so I excuse you. And I am now puzzling my head to find out how I am to prove what I have said about the superi-

ority of man, so as to make you understand
it."

Seaweed. " Then you admit there is a little
difficulty in proving it ?   Even *you* confess it
to be rather puzzling."

Bookworm. " I do ; but the difficulty does
not lie where you think it does.   I am sorry
to say it—but the only thing that prevents
your *understanding* the superiority of man
is, your own immeasurable inferiority to him !
However many mistakes he may make about
you, he can correct them all by a little closer
or more patient observation.   But no observation can make you understand what man is.
You are quite within the grasp of *his* powers,
but *he* is quite beyond the reach of *yours*."

Seaweed. " You are not over-civil, with all
your learning, Mr. Bookworm."

Bookworm. " I do not mean to be rude, I
assure you.   You are both of you very beautiful creatures, and, I dare say, very useful, too.
But you should not fancy either that you *do*
know everything, or that you are *able* to

9*

know everything.   And, above all, you should not dispute the superiority **and** powers of another creature merely because you cannot understand them."

Seaweed. " And am I then to believe all the long stories anybody may choose to come and tell me, about the wonderful powers of other creatures ?—and, when I inquire what those wonderful powers are, am I to be told that I can't understand them, but am to believe them all the same as if I did ? "

Bookworm. " Certainly not, unless the wonderful powers are proved by wonderful results ; but if they are, I advise you to believe in them whether you understand them or not."

Seaweed. " I should like to know how I am to believe what I don't understand."

Bookworm. " Very well, then, don't ! and remain an ignorant fool all your life. Of course you can't *really* understand anything but what is within the narrow limits of your own powers ; so, if you choose to make those powers the limits of your belief, I wish you joy, for you certainly won't be overburdened with knowledge."

Seaweed. "I will retort upon you that it is very easy to be contemptuous to your inferiors, Mr. Bookworm. You would do much better to try and explain to me those wonderful powers themselves, and so remove all the difficulties that stand in the way of my belief."

Bookworm. "If I were to try ever so much, I should not succeed. You can't understand even *my* superiority."

Seaweed. "Oh, Bookworm! now you are growing conceited!"

Bookworm. "Indeed I am not; but you shall judge for yourself. I can do many things you can't do ; among others, I can *see.*"

Seaweed. "What is that ? "

Bookworm. "There, now ! I knew I should puzzle you, directly! Why, seeing is something that I do with a very curious machine in my head, called an eye. But as you have not got an eye, and therefore cannot see, how am I to make you understand what seeing is ? "

Seaweed. "Why, you can tell us, to be sure."

Bookworm. "Tell you what? I can tell you I see. I can say, *Now I see, now I see,* as I walk over you and see the little bits of you that fall under my small eye. Indeed, I can also tell you *what* I see ; but how will that teach you what seeing is? You have got no eye, and therefore also you can never know what seeing is."

Zoöphyte. "Then why need we believe there is such a thing as seeing ? "

Bookworm. " Oh, pray, don't believe it ! I don't know why you should, I am sure ! There's no harm at all in being ignorant and narrow-minded. I am sure I had much rather you took no further trouble in the matter ; for you are, both of you, very testy and tire-some. It is from nothing but pride and vanity, too, after all. You want to be in a higher place in creation than you are put in, and no good ever comes of that. If you'd be content to learn wonderful things in the only way that is open to you, I should have a great deal of pleasure in telling you more."

Zoöphyte. " And pray, what way is that ? "

Bookworm. " Why, from the effects produced by them. As I said before, even where you cannot *understand* the wonderful powers themselves, you may have the grace to believe in their existence, from their wonderful results."

Seaweed. " And the results of what you call ' seeing ' are——"

" In man," interrupted the Bookworm, " that he gets to know everything about you, and all the creatures, and plants, and stones he looks at ; so that he knows your shape, and growth, and colour, and all about the cells of the little creatures that live in you— how many feelers they have, what they live upon, how they catch their food, how the eggs come out of the egg-cells, where you

live, where you are to be found, what other
Zoöphytes are related to you, which are most
like you,—in short, the most minute particu-
lars ;—so that he puts you into his collections,
not among strange creatures, but near to
those you are nearest related to ; and he
describes you, and makes pictures of you,
and gives you a name so that you are known
for the same creature, wherever you are found,
all over the world.   And now, I'm quite out
of breath with telling you all these wonderful
results of seeing."

"But he once took me for a vegetable,"
mused the Zoöphyte.

"Yes ; as I said before, he had not observed quite close enough, nor had he then
invented a curious instrument which enables
his great big eye to see such little fellows as
your inhabitants are.   But when he made
that instrument, and looked very carefully,
he saw all about you."

"Ay, but he still calls me an animal," observed the Seaweed.

"I know he does, but I am certain he will not do so long! If you are a vegetable, I will warrant him to find it out when he examines you a little more."

"You expect us to believe strange things, Bookworm," observed the Zoöphyte.

"To be sure, because there is no end of strange things for you to believe! And what you can't find out for yourself you must take upon trust from your betters," laughed the Bookworm. "It's the only plan. *Observation and* **Revelation** *are the sole means of acquiring knowledge.*"

Just at that moment the door opened, and two gentlemen entered the room.

"Ah, my new specimens on the floor!" observed the Naturalist; "but never mind," added he, as he picked them up, "here is the very one we wanted; it will serve admirably for our purpose. I shall only sacrifice a small branch of it, though." ·

And the Naturalist cut off a little piece of the Seaweed and laid it in a saucer, and

poured upon it some liquid from a bottle ;
and an effervescence began to take place forth-
with, and the Seaweed's limy coat began to
give way ; and the two gentlemen sat watching the result.

"Now," whispered the Bookworm to the
Zoöphyte, " those two men are looking closely
at your Seaweed friend, and trying what they
call experiments, that they may find out what
he is ; and if they do not succeed, I will
give up all my arguments in despair."

But they *did* succeed !

The gentlemen watched on till all the lime
was dissolved, and there was nothing left in
the saucer but a delicate red branch with
little round things upon it that looked like
tiny apples.

"This is the fruit, decidedly," remarked
the Naturalist ; "and now we will proceed
to examine it through the microscope."

And they did so.

And an hour or more passed, and a sort of
sleepy forgetfulness came over the Bookworm

and his two friends ; for they had waited till they were tired for further remarks from the Naturalist. And, therefore, it was with a start they were aroused at last by hearing him exclaim, "It is impossible to entertain the slightest doubt. If I ever had any, I have none now ; and the *corallines* must be removed back once more to their position among vegetables !"

The Naturalist laughed as he loosened the gum from the specimen, which he placed on a fresh paper, and classed among Red Sea-weeds. And soon after, the two gentlemen left the room once more.

"So he has really found our friend out !" cried the Zoöphyte ; and he was right about the fruit, too. Oh, Bookworm, Bookworm ! would that I could know what *seeing* is !"

"Oh, Zoöphyte, Zoöphyte ! I wish you would not waste your time in struggling after the unattainable ! You know what *feeling* is. Well, I would tell you that *seeing* is something of the same sort as feeling, only that it is quite different. Will that do ?"

" It sounds like nonsense."

" It *is* nonsense.   There *can* be no answer but nonsense, if you want to understand ' really for a fact,' as you call it, powers that are above you.   Explain to the rock on which you grow, what *feeling* is !"

" How could I ?" said the Zoöphyte ? " it has no sensation."

" No more than you have sight," rejoined the Bookworm.

" That is true, indeed," cried the Zoöphyte. " Bookworm ! I am satisfied—humbled, I must confess, but satisfied.   And now I will rejoice in our position here, glory in our new master, and admire his wonderful powers, even while I cannot understand them."

" I am proud of my disciple," returned the Bookworm, kindly.

" I also am one of them," murmured the Seaweed ; " but tell me, now, are there any other strange powers in man ?"

" Several," was the Bookworm's answer : " but to be really known they must be possessed. A lower power cannot compass the full understanding of a higher. But to limit one's belief to the bounds of one's own small powers, would be to tie one's self down to the foot of a tree, and deny the existence of its upper branches."

"There are no powers beyond those that man possesses, I suppose," mused the Zoö-phyte.

"I am far from saying that," replied the Bookworm ; "on the contrary——"

But what he would have said further no one knows, for once more the door opened, and the Naturalist, who now returned alone, spent his evening in putting by the specimens in their separate volumes on the shelves. And it was a long, long time before the Bookworm saw them again ; for the volumes in which they were kept were bound in Russia leather, to the smell of which he had a particular dislike, so that he never could make his way to them for a friendly chat again.

VI.

𝔗𝔥𝔢 𝔏𝔦𝔤𝔥𝔱 𝔬𝔣 𝔗𝔯𝔲𝔱𝔥.

"We know that all things work together for good.—Rom. vii. 28.

"DETESTABLE phantom!" cried the traveller, as his horse sank with him into the morass; "to what a miserable end have you lured me, by your treacherous light!"

"The same old story forever!" muttered the Will-o'-the-Wisp, in reply. "Always throwing blame on others for troubles you have brought upon yourself. What more could have been done for you, unhappy creature, than I have done? All the weary night through have I danced on the edge of this morass, to save you and others from ruin.

If you have rushed in further and further, like a headstrong fool, in spite of my warning light, who is to blame but yourself?"

"I *am* an unhappy creature, indeed ;" rejoined the traveller : "I took your light for a friendly lamp, but have been deceived, to my destruction."

"Yet not by *me*," cried the Will-o'-the-Wisp, anxiously. I work out my appointed business carefully and ceaselessly. My light is ever a friendly lamp to the wise. It misleads none but the headstrong and ignorant."

"Headstrong! ignorant!" exclaimed the Statesman, for such the traveller was. "How little do you know to whom you are speaking! Trusted by my King—honored by my country—the leader of her councils—ah, my country, my poor country! who will take my place and guide you when I am gone?"

"A guide who cannot guide himself! Misjudging, misled, and—though wise, perhaps, in the imperfect laws of society—ignorant in the glorious laws of Nature and of

10*

Truth—who will miss you, presumptuous being? You have mistaken the light that warned you of danger for the star that was to
guide you to safety. Alas for your country,
if no better leader than you can be found!"

The Statesman never spoke again, and
the Will-o'-the-Wisp danced back to the
edge of the black morass ; and as he flicker-
ed up and down, he mourned his luckless fate
—always trying to do good—so often vilified
and misjudged. "Yet," said he to himself,
as he sent out his beams through the cheer-
less night, "I will not cease to try ; who
knows but that I may save *somebody* yet!
But what an ignorant world I live in !"

* * * * * *

" Cruel monster !" shrieked the beautiful
Girl, in wild despair, as her feet plunged into
the swamp, and she struggled in vain to find
firmer ground, "you have betrayed me to
my death !"

"Ay, ay, I said so! It is always some
one else who is to blame, and never your-

selves, when pretty fools like you deceive themselves. You call me 'monster'—why did you follow a 'monster' into a swamp?" cried the poor Will-o'-the-Wisp, angrily.

"I thought my betrothed had come out to meet me. I mistook your hateful light for his. Oh, cruel fiend, I know you now! Must I die so young, so fair? Must I be torn from life, and happiness, and love? Ay, dance! dance on, in your savage joy."

"Fool as you are, it is no joy to me to see you perish," answered the Will-o'-the-Wisp. "It is my appointed law to warn and save those who will be warned. It is my appointed sorrow, I suppose, that the recklessness and ignorance of such as you, persist in disregarding that law, and turning good into evil. I shone bright and brighter before you as you advanced, entreating you. as it were, to be warned. But, in wilfulness. you pursued me to your ruin. What cruel mother brought you up, and did not teach you to distinguish the steady beam that guides to happiness, from the wandering brilliancy that bodes destruction?"

"My poor mother!" wept the Maiden; "what words are these you speak of her? But you, in your savage life, know nothing of what she has done for me, her only child. Mistress of every accomplishment that can adorn and delight society, my lightest word, my very smile, is a law to the world we move in."

"Even so! Accomplished in fleeting and fantastic arts that leave no memorial behind them—unacquainted with the beauty and purposes of the realities around you, which work from age to age in silent mercy for gracious ends, and put to shame the toil that has no aim or end. Oh, that you had but known the law by which I live!"

The Maiden spoke no more, and then she ceased to struggle. The Will-o'-the-Wisp danced back yet another time to the edge of the black morass; "for," said he, "I may

save somebody yet.   But what a foolish world
I live in!"

*   *   *   *   *

" The old Squire should mend these here
roads," observed Hobbinoll the farmer to his
son Colin, as they drove slowly home from
market in a crazy old cart, which shook about
with such jerks that little Colin tried in vain
to keep curled up in a corner.   It was hard
to say whether the fault was most in the
roads,—though they were rather rutty, it
must be owned,—or in the stumbling old pony
who went from side to side, or in the not
very sober driver, who seemed unable at
times to distinguish the reins apart, so that
he gave sudden pulls, first one way and then
the other.   But through all these troubles it
comforted the Farmer's heart to lay all the
blame on the Squire for the bad roads that
led across the boggy moor.   Colin, however,
took but little interest in the matter ; but at
length, when a more violent jerk than usual
threw him almost sprawling on the bottom of

the cart, he jumped up, laid hold of the side planks, and began to look around him with his half-sleepy eyes, trying to find out where they were. At last he said, " She's coming, father."

" Who's coming ?" shouted Hobbinoll.

" T' mother," answered Colin.

" What's she coming for, I wonder," said Hobbinoll ; " we've enough in the cart without her."

" But you're going away from her, Father," expostulated Colin, half-crying. " I see her with the lantern, and she'll light us home. You can't see, Father ; let me have the reins." But Hobbinoll refused to give up the reins, though he was not very fit to drive. In the struggle, however, he caught sight of the light which Colin took for his mother's lantern.

" And is *that* the fool's errand you'd be going after ?" cried he, pointing with his whip to the light. " It's lucky for you, young one, you have not had the driving of us home to-night, though you think you can do anything, I know. A precious home it would have been, at the **bottom of** the sludgy pool yonder, for that's where you'd have got us to at last. Yon light is the Will-o'-the-Wisp, **that's always trying to mislead folks.** Bad luck befal him! I got half-way to him once when I was a young'un, but **an old** neighbour who'd once been in himself was **going by** just then, and called me back. He's a villain is **that** sham-faced **Will-o'-the-Wisp.**"

With these **words the Farmer struck** the pony so harshly with **his heavy** whip, twitching the reins convulsively at the same time, at the mere memory of **his adv**enture in the bog, that little Colin was thrown up and down **like a** ball, and the cart rolled forward in and out of the ruts **at such** a pace, that Hobbinoll got home to his wife sooner than she ever dared to hope for **on** market evenings.

"They are safe," observed the Will-o'-the-Wisp, as the cart moved **on,** "and that is the great point gained! Nevertheless, such wisdom is mere brute experience. In their ignorance they would have struck the hand that helped them. Nevertheless, I will try again, for I may yet save some one else. But what a rude and ungrateful world I live in!"

*   *   *   *   *

"I see a light at last, papa!" shouted a little Boy on a Shetland pony, as he rode by his Father's side along the moor. "I am so glad! There is either a cottage, or a friendly man with a lantern who will help us to find our way. Let me go after him; I can soon overtake him." And the little Boy touched his pony with a whip, and in another minute would have been cantering along after the light, but that his Father laid a sudden and heavy hand upon the bridle.

"Not a step further in *that* direction, at any rate, if you please, my darling."

"Oh, Papa!" expostulated the child, pointing with his hand to the light.

And, "Oh, my son, I see!" cried the Father, smiling; "and well is it for you that I not only see, but know the meaning of what I see at the same time. That light is neither the gleam from a cottage, nor yet a friendly man with a lantern, as you think, though, for the matter of that, the light is friendly enough to those who understand it. It shines there to warn us from the dangerous part of the bog. Kind old Will-o'-the-Wisp! pursued the Father, raising his voice, as if calling through the darkness into the distance—"Kind old Will-o'-the-Wisp, we know what you mean; we will not come near your deadly swamps. The old Naturalist knows you well—good night, and thank you for the warning." So saying, the Naturalist turned the reins of his son's pony the other way, and they both trotted along, keeping the beaten road as well as they could by the imperfect light.

"After all, it was more like a lantern than those pictures of the nasty Will-o'-the-Wisp, Papa," murmured the little Boy, reluctantly urging his pony on.

"Our friend is not much indebted to you for the pretty name you have called him," laughed the Father. "You are of the same mind as the poet, who, with the licence of his craft, said—

'Yonder phantom only flies
  To lure thee to thy doom.'"

"Yes, Papa, and so he does," interposed the Boy.

"But, indeed, he does no such thing, my dear,—on the contrary, he spends all his life in shining brightly to warn travellers of the most dangerous parts of the swamp."

"But the shining seems as if he was inviting them to go after him, Papa."

"Only because you choose to think so, my dear, and do not inquire. Does the sailor think the shining of the lighthouse invites him to approach the dangerous rocks on which it is built?"

"Oh, no, Papa, because he knows it is put there on purpose to warn him away."

"He only knows by teaching and inquiry, Arthur ; and so you, also, by teaching and inquiry, will learn to know that this Will-o'-the-Wisp is made to shine for us in swamps and marshes as a land-beacon of danger. The laws of Nature, which are the acted will of God, work together in this case, as in all others, for a good end. And it is given to us as both a privilege and a pleasure to search them out and to avail ourselves of the mercies, whilst we admire the wonders of the great Creator. Can you think of a better employment?"

The fire was very bright, and the tea was warm and good, that greeted the travellers, Father and Son, on their arrival at home that night. Many a joke, too, passed with Mamma as to the sort of tea they should have tasted, and the kind of bed they should have lain down in, had they only gone after the Will-o'-the-Wisp, as young Arthur had so much wished to do.

And for just a few days after these events —not more, for children's wisdom seldom does, or ought to, last much longer—Arthur

11

had every now and then a wise and philosophical fit, and on the principle that, however much appearances might be to the contrary, the laws of Nature were always working to some good and beneficent end, he sagely and gravely reproved his little sister for crying when a shower of hailstones fell; "for surely," said he, "though we cannot go out to-day, the storm is doing good to something or somebody, somewhere."

It was a blessed creed! though it cost him a struggle to adhere to it when the lightning flashed round him, and the thunder roared in the distance, and he saw from the windows dark clouds hanging over the landscape. When some one said the storm had been very grand, he thought—yes, but it was grander still to think that all these laws of Nature, as they are called,—this acted will of God,— was forever working, night and day, in darkness and in light, recognised or unheeded, for some wise and beneficent end.

Yes! when he was older he would try and trace out these ends—a better employment

could not be found.   And it may be, that in
long after years, when the storms and the
clouds that gathered round him were harder
yet to look through, because they were men-
tal troubles; it may be, that then, from
amidst the tender recollections of his infancy,
the gleaming of the Will-o'-the-Wisp would
suddenly rise and shine before him with comfort.   For the Student of Nature who had
traced so many blessed ends out of dark and
mysterious beginnings, held fast to the humil-
ity and faith of childhood ; and where his
mind was unable to penetrate, his heart was
contented to believe.   *   *   *

Meanwhile the Will-o'-the-Wisp had heard
the kind good-night that greeted him as the
travellers passed by on that dark evening.
And his light shone brighter than ever, as he
said, " I am happy, now.   I have saved the
life of one who not only is thankful for it,
but knows the hand that saved him."   With
these words he cheerily danced back again
to his appointed post.

11*

VII.

𝔚𝔞𝔦𝔱𝔦𝔫𝔤.

———

"It is good that a man should both hope and quietly wait."
LAM. iii. 26.

T was, doubtless, a very sorry life the House Cricket led, before houses were built and fires were kindled. There was no comfortable kitchen hearth, then, in the warm nooks and corners of which he might sit and sing his cheerful song, coming out every now and then to bask himself in the glow of the blazing light. On the contrary, he, so fond of heat, had no place to shelter in but holes in hollow trees, or crevices in rocks and stones, or some equally dull and damp abode. Besides which, he had to bear the incessant taunts

[126]

and ridicule of creatures who were perfectly comfortable themselves, and so had no fellow-feeling for his want of cheerfulness.

"Why don't you go and spring about, and sing in the fields with your cousin, the Grasshopper?" was the ill-natured question of the Spider, as she twisted her web in one of the refuge-holes the Cricket had crept into ; "I am sure your legs are long enough, if you would only take the trouble to undouble them. It's nothing but a sulky, discontented feeling that keeps you and all your family moping in these out-of-the-way corners, when you ought to be using your limbs in jumping about and enjoying yourself. And I dare say, too, that you could sing a great deal louder if you chose."

The Cricket thought, perhaps he could,—but he must feel very differently to what he did then, before it would be possible to try. Something was so very, very wrong with him, but what that something was he did not know. All the other beasts and birds and

insects seemed easy and happy enough. The
Spider, for instance, was quite at home and
gay in the hole *he* found so dismal. And it
was not the Spider only who was contented :
the Flies—the Bees—the Ants—the very
Mole, who sometimes came up from burrow-
ing, and told wonderful stories of his under-
ground delights—the Birds, with their merry
songs—the huge Beasts, who walked about
like giants in the fields—all—all were satisfied with their condition, and happy in them
selves. Every one had the home he liked,
and no one envied the other.

But with him it was quite otherwise ; he
never felt at home ! on the contrary, it always seemed to him that he was looking out
for something that was not there—some place
that could never be found—some state where
he could rise out of the depression and un-
easiness which here seemed to clog him down,
though he could not understand why. Poor
fellow ! as things were now, he felt forever
driven to hide in holes, although he knew

that his limbs were built for energy ; and few ever heard his voice, though he possessed one fitted for something much better than doleful complaints.

Sometimes a set of House Crickets would meet, and talk the matter over. They looked at their long, folded-up legs, and could not but see how exactly they were like those of the Grasshopper. And yet the idea of following the Grasshopper into the cool grass, and jumping about all day, was odious to them. Once, indeed, a Cricket of great self-denial offered to go into the fields and find one of his green cousins, and ask his opinion on the subject, and whether he could give any reason why the grasshopper life should be so distasteful to such near relations. And he actually went ; and when the Grasshopper could be persuaded to stand quiet for a few seconds, and listen, he was so much concerned for the Crickets (for he had a tender heart, from living so much in the grass, and being so musical), that he said he would himself visit his cousins, and see what could be done for them. Perhaps it was some little accidental ailment, or it might be a chronic affection in the family, owing to mismanagement when they were young, but which a little judicious treatment would correct.

With these views he started for the hollow tree in which the Crickets had taken shelter, and soon reached it,—for he travelled the whole way in bounds. And the last bound took him fairly into the midst of the family circle, in which indeed he alighted with more vivacity than politeness, for his cousins did not like such startling gaiety. However, he steadied himself carefully, and then began to examine the legs and knees of all the Crickets assembled. He drew them out, and looked them well over; for, thought he, "there is perhaps some blunder or flaw in the way the joints are put together." But he could find nothing amiss. There sat the Crickets, with legs and bodies as nicely made as his own, only with no energy for exertion.

What he might have thought, or what he might have said, after this puzzling discovery, no one can tell ; for at the end of his examination he was seized with the fidgets, and, " Excuse me, my dear friends," cried he ; " I have the cramp in my left leg—I *must* jump ! " And jump he did—once, twice, thrice—and the last jump carried him out of the tree ; and either on purpose, or from forgetfulness, he sprang singing away, and returned to his cousins the Crickets no more.

Oh, this yearning after some other better state that lies unrevealed in the indefinite future—how restless and disheartening a sensation ! Oh, this painful contrast of perfection in all created things around, to the lonely meditator on so much happiness, who is the solitary exception to the rule—how trying the position ! How cruel, how almost overwhelming the struggle between the iron chain of reality and the soaring wing of aspiration !

But, " What is the use, my poor good

friends," expostulated a plodding old Mole,
one day, after coming out to see how the
upper world went on, and hearing the Cricket's complaints—" what is the use of all this
groaning and conjecturing ? You admit
that every other creature but yourself is
perfect in its way, and quite happy. Well,
then, I will tell you that you ought to be
quite sure you are perfect in your way, too,
though you have not found it out yet; and
that you will be happy one day or other,
although it may not be the case just now.
Do you suppose this fine scheme of things we
live in is to be soiled with one speck of dirt,
as it were for the sake of teasing such a little
insignificant creature as yourself? Don't
think it for a moment, for it is not at all
likely ! But you must not suppose that
everything goes right at first, even with the
best of us. I have had some small experience,
and I know. But everything fits in at last.
Of that I am quite sure. For instance, now,
I do not suppose it ever occurred to you to

think what a trial it must be to a young
Mole when he first begins to burrow in the
earth. Do you imagine that he knows what
he is doing it for, or what **will** be the result?
No such thing. It is a complete working in
the dark, not knowing in the least where he
is going. Dear me! if one had once stopped
to conjecture and puzzle, what a hardship it
would have seemed to drive one's nose by
the hour together into unknown ground, for
some unexplained reason that did not come
out for some time afterwards, and that one
had no certainty would ever come out at all!
But everything fits in at last. And so **it** did
with us. I remember it quite well in my
own case. We drove the earth away and
outwards, till the space so cleared proved an
absolute palace!—By-the-by, I must try and
get you down into our splendid abode—it
will cheer you up, and teach you a useful
lesson.—Well, so you see we found out at
last what all the grubbing had been for——"

"Ah! but," interrupted the Cricket, "you

12

were labouring for *some* purpose all the time,
and if· I had to labour I could hope. The
difficulty is, to sit moping, with nothing to do
but *wait.*"

" It is nonsense to talk of nothing to do,"
answered the Mole ; " every creature has
something to do. You, for instance, have
always to watch for the sun. You know
you like the beams and warmth he sends out
better than anything else in the world,—so
you should get into the way of them as much
as you can. And after the sun has set, you
must hunt up the snuggest holes you can find,
and so make the best of things as they are ;
and for the rest, you must *wait.* And waiting answers sometimes as well as working, I
can assure you. There was the young Ox in
the plains near here. As soon as he could
run about at all, he began driving his clumsy
head against everything he met.* No one

---

*"The bull-calf butts with smooth and unarmed brow,
.   .   .   .   and no pre-assurance common to a whole
species does in any instance prove delusive."—Coleridge's
Aids to Reflection.

could tell why ; but he fidgeted and butted
about all day long, and many of his friends
and acquaintance were very much offended
by his manners. Others laughed. The dogs,
indeed, were particularly amused, and used
to bark at him constantly—even close to his
nose, sometimes, as he lowered his head after
them. Well, at last out came the secret.
Two fine horns grew out from our friend's
head, and people soon understood the meaning of all the butting ; and one of the saucy
curs who was playing the old barking game
with him one day, got finely tossed for his
pains. Everything fits in at last, my friends !
No cravings are given in vain. There is
always something in store to account for
them, you may be quite sure. You *may*
have to wait a bit- -some of you a shorter,
some a longer time ; but *do* wait-—and everything will fit in and be perfect at last."

It was a most **fortunate** circumstance for
the Crickets that the Mole happened to give
them this good advice ; for a malicious Ape

had lately been suggesting to them, whether, as they were totally useless and very unhappy, it would not be a good thing for them all to starve themselves to death, or in some other way to rid the world of their whole race. But the Mole's good sense gave a different turn to their ideas; and hope is so natural and pleasant a feeling, that when once they ventured to encourage it, it flourished and grew in their hearts till it created a sort of happiness of itself. In short, they determined to *wait*, and meantime to watch for the sun, as their friend had advised.

There are not many records of the early history of the House Crickets; but it is supposed that they travelled about a good deal— preferring always the hottest countries; and rumours of a few straggling families who had discovered a sort of Cricket Elysium at the mouth of volcanoes, were afloat at one time. But the truth of the report was never ascertained: and as, doubtless, if ever they got there, they were sure to be swept away to destruction by the first eruption that took place, it is no wonder that the fact has never been thoroughly established.

Meanwhile, several generations died off; and things remained much as they were. But the words of the Mole were carried down from father to son, and became a by-word of comfort among them :—" Everything would fit in at last! no cravings are given in vain. There is always something in store to account for them. *Wait*—and everything will fit in, and be perfect at last."

Gleams of hope, indeed, were not wanting to our poor little friends, during this time of probation. Wherever fires were kindled by human hands, whether by wanderers in the depths of forests, or sojourners in tents, a stir of excitement and rapturous expectation was caused among such Crickets as were near enough to know and enjoy the circumstance. But, alas! when the travellers journeyed onwards, or the tents were removed elsewhere, the disappointment that ensued was bitter in proportion.

Many an evil hint, too, had they on such occasions from the mischief-making creatures which are to be found in all grades of life, that such, and no better, would be their fate forever. Rays of joy, beaming only to be extinguished in cruel mockery of their feelings —such was to be their perpetual portion!

"But we *will* not believe it," cried the Crickets, heart-broken as they were. "Everything will be perfect at last," sang they as loudly as they could. "No cravings are given in vain." And as they always sang this same song, the mischief-makers got tired of listening at last, and left them to sing and weep alone. Ah! it required no small strength of mind to resist, as they did, such plausible insinuations, supported as they were by present appearances.

But, truly, though it tarried, the day of deliverance and joy did come! The first fire that ever warmed the hearthstone that flagged

the grand old chimney arch of ancient times,
ended for ever the mystery of the House
Crickets' wants and cravings ; and when it
commonly blazed every winter night in men's
dwellings, all the doubts and woes of Cricket
life were over. These seemed to have passed
away like the dreams of a disturbed night,
which had been succeeded by daylight and
reality. And oh, what ecstasy of joy the
Crickets felt! How loud they shouted,
and how high they sprang! "We knew it
would be so! The good old Mole was right!
The grumbling beasts were wrong! Everything is perfect now, and no one is so happy
as we are."

"Grandmother, what creature is it that I
hear singing so loudly in the corner by the
fire?" inquires the little one of the good old
dame who sits musing on the oaken settle.

"I do not hear it, my child, and I do not
know," answers the deaf and blind old crone.
"But if it be singing, love, it is happy, and
enjoys these blessed fires as much as I do.

'Let everything that hath breath praise the Lord.'"

Ah! it was no wonder that amidst the many merry voices that then shouted, and still shout, round those warm and friendly fires, no voice is louder, no joy more grateful, than that of the patient Cricket. He has "waited" through fear and shadows—has hoped through darkness and ignorance—and his abode now glows with warmth and light. And, if he received a lesson of wisdom from a creature more humble and seemingly more blind than himself, it is at least not the only instance in which instruction has been so obtained.

And now we know the reason why the Crickets come by troops into our houses, and live and thrive about our cheering fires, and sing so loud and long that the housewives sometimes (I grieve to say) get weary of the noise, and try to lessen the number of their lively visitors. But yet there is a strange, old notion of good fortune attending the presence of these little chirping creatures. They are welcomed as bringing "good luck" to the family about whose hearth they settle. And so they do! They bring with them a tale of promises made good. They sing a song of hope fulfilled ; and though in that glad music there be neither speech nor language which we can recognize as such, there is yet a voice to be heard among them by all who love to listen, with reverent delight, to the sweet harmonies and deep analogies of nature.

VIII.

A Lesson of Hope.

―

"Oh, yet we trust that, somehow, good
Will be the final goal of ill!"
From TENNYSON'S "*In Memoriam.*"

"NOW the rising blast is driving through the ancient forest! What a dismal roaring there is among the pine-trees! What a sharp clattering among the half-dried poplar-leaves! What a sighing among the beeches! A wild, mysterious hour, and full of strange, fantastic types of mortal life!"

It was thus I spoke, when, having wandered out one gloomy autumn night to muse on Nature and her laws, I found myself contemplating, in the deep recesses of a wood,

[142]

the progress of a violent storm. And as I paused, I leant **back, in** sad reflections lost, against an oak, **and,** looking upwards to the sky, tried to gaze into the depths of those black vapoury masses that **had** arisen, one knew not how or whence, to darken over the expanse of heaven, when all **at** once there shone down upon **me, from** an opening in the clouds, the full rays of **a** bright October moon.

The light was sudden, and a sudden revulsion took place within my heart. I had been thinking that, like the cruel storm, and like the heavy clouds, were the troubles and the trials **of** human existence ; and now, when that sweet radiance broke upon my eyes, I heard a voice exclaim, as if in echo to my thoughts—" It is the moon that shone **in** Paradise !" It was the Bird of Night, quite near me, in the hollow of a tree. Looking to see from whence the sound had come, I met his large, grave, meditative eyes fixed on my moonlit face, and then I heard the voice exclaim again—"The moon that shone in Paradise !"

Oh, what a thought to come across the tumult of that hour ! *The moon that shone in Paradise !*—up to whose radiant orb the eyes of countless generations have been turned —from the first glance of spotless innocence to the last yearning gaze of sorrow-stricken manhood ! And why ?—but that in that calm, unchanging **glory** there shines forth a promise of eternal, everlasting peace. But now another voice was heard, despite the howling of the storm. It was a croaking Raven, swinging on a branch beside me. He came between me and the light, and ever and anon his coal-black wings seemed spreading for a flight.

" Deluded fool," he muttered, " with your endless myths ! This comes of living in the dark all day, and spending all your time in guess-work ! See ! your precious moon is gone !"

" Not gone, though hidden," was the answer.

But I heard no more than this, for here the frightful **wind grew** louder still. He roared in fury all around, scattering the last leaves from the bending trees, **as if he hated** the **very** relics of the **gentle summer.** And many bowed their heads, and others moaned in grief.

"Hast thou **come** with mighty news from distant lands," shouted the Pine-tree, scornfully, as he tossed his branches **to the storm,** "that thou bringest such confusion in thy path? Ambassador of **evil! who has** sent thee here?"

"Cannot yonder moon teach thee milder thoughts?" cried the Elm-tree, as he stood, majestic in his sorrow and despair.

"Our hour is come," exclaimed the softer Beech. "**My** leaves lie scattered all around. Our life is closing fast. Naked and forlorn we stand, amid the ruins of the past."

"What mockery of existence," stormed the black-leaved Poplar, in his wrath, "to be placed here, and clothed in such sweet beauty, nurtured by gentle dews and tender sunshine, and then be left at last the victims of reckless fury, with all our glories torn by force away! Would I had never risen from the ground!"

"Oh, my aspiring friend," the ill-mouthed Raven cried, "the few months' splendour does not satisfy your heart! You aim too high, methinks. Well, well! aspiring thoughts are very fine; but were I you I would accommodate myself to facts. A short spring, a shorter summer, and then to perish. Ha! here you are again, my ancient, worthy friend?"

And then another gust broke in with savage fury on the forest, and many a stalwart branch crashed down upon the ground. The wailings of afflicted nature rose amidst the storm.

"Is there no refuge from this end?" inquired the Oak. "Why have I lived at all?"

"Because destruction is the law of life," the Raven uttered, with his fiercest croak.

" Where would destruction be, were there no life to be destroyed ? It is a glorious law."

" No law, but only an exception," cried the Bird of Night.

And as he spoke there streamed once more from out **the clouds that** type of peace that passeth not away—the moon that shone in Paradise. Oh, what a silver mantle she let fall upon the disrobed branches of those trees ! Wet as they were with rain-drops, and waving in the gale, it seemed as if **they** shone in robes of starlight glory. What gracious promises seemed streaming down with that sweet light !

" Lift up your heads, ye forest trees, once more ;" so sang the mild-eyed Bird of Night. " Fury is short-lived—love alone enduring. All that destroys is transitory, but order is everlasting. The unbridled powers of cruelty may rage—it is but for a time ! **And ye** may darken over the blue heavens, ye vapoury masses in the sky. It matters not ! Beyond the howling of that wrath, beyond the blackness of those clouds, there shines, unaltered and serene, the moon that shone in Paradise."

"Your myth again, detested Bird of Night! Here, to the rescue, ancient friend!"

And louder then than ever came that cruel, cruel wind.

"It matters not," once more the Owl exclaimed. "The stormy winds must cease, the clouds must pass away, and yonder sails the light that tells of harmony restored."

"Infatuated fool, to live on hope, with death around you and before you!" groaned the Raven—and then a crash like thunder rent the air. The Oak had fallen to the ground. I started at the shock.

"Will the day ever come," I cried aloud, as if addressing some mysterious friend, "will the day ever come when storms and woe shall cease? Order and peace seem meant, but death and ruin come to pass."

"Oh, miserable doubter, do you ask? Must the brute beasts and mute creation rise to give an answer to your fears? Look in the heaven above, and in the earth below, and in the water deep beneath the earth. One only law is given—the law of order, harmony and joy."

" Alas, how often broken," I exclaimed.

" Ay, but disturbance is no law, and therefore cannot last. Disorder, death, destruction : by their own nature they are transitory ; rebellious powers that struggle for a time, and frustrate here and there the gracious purposes ordained. But they exist not of themselves ; have neither law nor being of themselves ; exist as but disturbers of a scheme whose deep foundations cannot be overthrown. Life, order, harmony and peace; means duly fitting ends ; the object, universal joy. This is the law. Believe in it, and live!"

And as the voice grew silent, from the sky beamed over all the scene the placid moon once more. The wind had lulled, or passed away to other regions of the earth, and over all the forest streamed the brilliant light.

13*

Once more the lit-up trees shone spangled o'er with rays; and happy murmurs broke upon my ear, instead of loud complaints.

" **We have been wild and foolish,** gracious Moon!" exclaimed the tender Beech. "We doubted all the promises and hopes you shed **so freely** down. In pity to the terrors of the night, forgive us once again!"

" **Y**ou have said right, my sister," said the Oak. "That heavenly power, whom neither winds nor storms can reach, will view with tenderness our troubled lot, who live amid the tempests of the earth. She will forgive, she hath forgiven us all. Hath she not clothed us now with robes more brilliant than the summer ones we love?"

"The robes of hope and promise," wept the Poplar, as he spoke; for all his branches trembled with delight, and stars seemed dropping all around.

"I mourn my dark despair," bewailed the Elm. I should have called the past to memory! We never are deserted in our need.

The winter tempests rage, and terrible they are ; but always the bright moon from time to time returns, to shed down rays of hope and promises of glory on our heads ; and still we doubt and fear, and still the patient moon repeats her tale. And then the spring and summer time return, and life, and joy, and all our beauteous robes. Oh. what weak tremblers we must be !"

And so, through all the rest of that strange night, murmurs of comfort sounded through the wood, and I returned at last to the poor, lonely cottage that I called my home, and wept mixed tears of sorrow and of joy. Father and mother lost, swept suddenly away, and I, with straitened means, left alone to struggle through the world ! Did I not stand before my desolate hearth, like one awakened from a dream, a vision—(surely, such it was !)—exclaiming in despair, as did the weeping Beech, " Naked and forlorn I stand, amid the ruins of the past." But through the casement glided in on me, me

also, as I stood, the blessed rays of that eter·
nal moon—the moon that shone in Paradise
—the moon that promises a Paradise restored.

And ever and anon, throughout the struggle of my life, I would return for wisdom and
for hope to the old forest where I dreamt
the dream. As time passed no, and winter
snows came down, a cold unmeaning sleep
seemed to bind up the trees—but still, at
her appointed time, the moon came out, and
lit up even snow with robes of light and
hope. And then the spring-time burst the
cruel bonds that held all nature in a stag-
nant state. Verdure and beauty came again;
and, as I listened to the gales that breathed
soft music through the trees, I thought, " If I
could dream again, I should hear songs of
exquisite delight." But that was not to be.
Still, I could revel in the comfort of the
sight, and watch the moonbeams glittering
in triumphant joy through the now verdant
bowers of those woods, playing in happy
sport amid the shadows of the leaves.

And to me also came a spring! From me, passed away the winter and its chill! And now I take the children of my love, and the sweet mother who has borne them, to those woods ; and ever and anon we tell long tales of Nature and her ways, and how the poor trees moan, when storms and tempests come ; and how the wise Owl talks to heedless ears his deep philosophy of laws of order that must one day certainly prevail, and how the patient moon is never weary of her task of shedding rays of hope and promise on the world ; and even while we speak, the children clap their hands for joy, and say they never will despair for anything that comes, for, lo! above their heads there suddenly shines out—THE **MOON THAT SHONE IN PAR-ADISE !**

www.ingramcontent.com/pod-product-compliance
Lightning Source LLC
Chambersburg PA
CBHW031119020726
47495CB00007B/2268